Between

a Tales of Moonspell novel

Jessica Coulter Smith

Printed in the United States of America

ALL RIGHTS RESERVED. No part of this book may be reproduced, stored in a retrieval system, or transmitted, in any form or by any means, without the prior permission in writing of the publisher, nor be otherwise circulated in any form of binding or cover other than that in which it is published and without a similar condition including this condition being imposed on the subsequent purchaser.

Publisher's Note: This is a work of fiction. All characters, places, businesses, and incidents are from the author's imagination. Any resemblance to actual places, people, or events is purely coincidental.

Cover by Jessica Coulter Smith

© 2012, Jessica Coulter Smith

Other Books by Jessica Coulter Smith

Whispering Lake
Magnolia Magick
Eternally Mine
Yuletide Spirit
Night's Embrace

Luna Werewolves series
Vicus Luna (Book 1)

Books in the Ashton Grove Series
Moonlight Protector (Book 1)
Moonlight Hero (Book 2)
Moonlight Guardian (Book 3)
Moonlight Champion (Book 4)
Moonlight Savior (Book 5)

Vaaden Captives
Sorcha
Enid
Susan

Vaaden Warriors
Rheul
Randar
Thale

Short Stories
For Now and Always
Creole Nights
Love at First Bite

I would like to say a special thank you to my husband for always believing in me.

Chapter One

Brandt and Nolen Fitzgerald surveyed the room. Most nights they'd have women crawling on them, but neither was interested in a quick fuck tonight. After seeing how happy their alpha was with his mate, it had made Brandt realize he wanted more than a string of one-night stands. Never had he seen two people more in love. He'd had fun, but at thirty-two it was time for him to actively look for his mate, and what better place than Luna del Morte? Very few humans came to the club, unless they were looking to be bitten by a vampire.

Having been part of the Moonspell pack his entire life, it was safe to say his mate wasn't a werewolf. Or if she was, she lived out of town. The thought that he'd have to wait for his mate to come to him or have to go searching for her was a disappointing one. Most of their friends had already paired off, and some either had children or were expecting. Brandt wasn't certain he was ready to face fatherhood, but he would jump in with both feet if that's what his mate wanted.

Of course, before he could contemplate that, he'd have to figure out their living arrangement. At the moment, he and Nolen shared the home their parents had left them. They hadn't discussed it, but as the oldest Brandt would probably keep the house, leaving Nolen to find his own home. But it had worked out well for them thus far.

More than once over the past few weeks they'd contemplated their relationships, such as they were -- Nolen had decided he was content with his single status, but Brandt was ready to find his mate, and Luna del Morte was his best option. Granted, he'd come to the conclusion his mate wasn't a werewolf, but he still hoped he didn't end up with a flighty fairy, or worse, a vampire. Surely his mate was a shapeshifter.

They scanned the dance floor -- Brandt looking for someone of interest and his brother lending a hand -- but neither brother had any luck. There were plenty of beautiful women around, but none called to them. Plenty gave them come-hither looks, but none sparked their interest. The night was young, however, so they didn't give up hope. Besides, Brandt wasn't counting on finding his special lady the first night out. He doubted he could be so lucky.

"How long do you think it will take?" Nolen asked.

"No telling. It could take days or months. Either way, I can't give up. If I don't find her here, we may have to visit some of the other packs. Most of our friends have found their mates."

"Yeah, but look how long it took Hayden," Nolen pointed out.

Brandt didn't want to contemplate another eight years without his mate, but it was always a possibility. Just because he was ready for his mate didn't mean he'd find her now. What if fate decided to punish him for his many one-night stands? If he were a woman, he'd would've been labeled a slut, same for Nolen.

"I have to believe I'll find her soon," he said. "I'm ready to move on with my life, and I can't do that without a mate."

"You know I'll help in any way I can."

Brandt nodded.

A group of women moving toward the dance floor drew their attention across the room. But it wasn't the scantily clad women who held their gazes. Just past them, sitting by herself, was a curvaceous woman in a modest black sleeveless top and jeans. Her foot tapped to the beat of the music, yet no one asked her to dance. Brown hair hung long and straight down her back and across one shoulder. Her skin was pale under the pulsing lights.

Both Brandt and Nolen stood at the same time.

"Where are you going?" Brandt asked.

"To dance."

Brandt followed his line of sight to the curvy woman. "Not with her you're not. I'm going to dance with her."

Nolen cocked his head to the side. "Why don't we both go dance with her?"

"She's not our usual type. What makes you think she'll go for it?" Brandt asked, thinking of the many women they'd shared over the years.

"Then we'll ask her one at a time. It's a shame for a woman like that to sit on the sidelines."

Brandt nodded. "Let's not overwhelm her. Wait here until you see us leaving the dance floor."

"You know, you're assuming she's going to say yes. What happens if she turns you down?" Nolen asked.

"She won't."

Brandt made his way through the crowd, getting stopped more than once by hopeful young women. At six foot four, Brandt was usually one of the taller men in a room. Add to that his tanned skin, black hair and blue eyes and he garnered more than his fair share of attention. Nolen, being his identical twin, also never lacked for female companionship. But at times like this, it was a curse.

He shouldered his way through and finally stood by her side. He could smell a tantalizing hint of jasmine in the air, and he knew it came from her. She looked up at him, her lips parting and her hazel eyes widening. Up close, she was stunning. Her lush curves filled out her clothes nicely, making him wonder what it would be like to cuddle her close at night. She was certainly a delightful handful.

"I saw you across the room," he said.

"*We* saw you," Nolen said, coming to stand behind him.

Brandt clenched his jaw. Why couldn't his brother ever follow instructions? It wasn't that he minded Nolen dancing with the beautiful woman, but he'd wanted a chance to be with her first.

Her eyes widened even more. "Both of you? At the same time?"

"No," Brandt said quickly. "Not at the same time. You'd dance with me first then my brother."

She looked back and forth between the two of them. "O-Okay."

"I'm Brandt and this is my brother Nolen."

"I'm Falan."

Brandt smiled and offered her his hand. Helping her to her feet, he wrapped an arm around her waist and led her onto the dance floor. A song he'd never heard before played, the beat making the very air vibrate with each note.

He pulled her close so that her body brushed against his with every movement. Her scent surrounded him and his wolf rumbled in pleasure. He leaned closer and sniffed, and he jolted in surprise. It seemed his wish had come true. He'd found his mate.

The song ended and they returned to the table. Nolen sat patiently waiting for his turn. Even knowing the woman was his mate, Brandt didn't mind his brother dancing with her. He just needed to make sure his twin knew to keep his hands to himself.

Leaning in close to Nolen, he whispered, "She's mine. I've found my mate."

His brother looked surprised but nodded his understanding. As Nolen put his hand on Falan's waist, Brandt was amazed to discover that he wasn't the slightest bit jealous. He didn't feel the urge to pull Falan back, or to growl at his brother. He'd always thought he'd feel proprietary toward his mate once he found her, but that didn't seem to be the case.

He watched the two of them dance, wishing he could join them. He had a feeling Falan wasn't used to being between two men. Just the thought that he was willing to share her, even if it was only on the dance floor, with his brother was rather baffling. He should want to wrap her up and hide her away where no one else could see her or touch her. So why didn't he feel that way? He knew without a doubt that she was his mate.

Falan and Nolen returned from dancing, a sparkle in his mate's eyes. He wondered how long she'd sat here tonight without anyone asking her to dance. While it was true, she was on the heavy side by today's standards, she was still the most beautiful woman he'd ever seen. All of those extra curves just meant he had more to hold onto when he made love to her.

His brother nudged him, drawing him from his thoughts. The look in Nolen's eyes worried him. It was too noisy on the dance floor for talking, so he knew his mate hadn't said anything to upset his brother.

"Falan, what are you drinking, baby?" Brandt asked.

"Strawberry margarita."

"We're going to get you a refill and we'll be right back."

She nodded and they turned to walked away.

Once they were alone, Brandt looked at his twin. "So what's bothering you?"

"It seems I've found my mate, too."

Brandt lifted a brow. "How? You only danced with Falan."

"Exactly."

He gave Nolen a blank look.

"We have the same mate!"

Brandt looked at Falan and back at his brother. "Are you sure?"

"Would I lie to you about something like this? Of course I'm sure."

"I don't think this is going to go over very well," Brandt said. "Something tells me she isn't into threesomes."

He paid for Falan's drink and they began walking back to her. She looked so lonely by herself. He wondered why she'd come to the club tonight. If she wasn't here with friends, had she hoped to meet someone? Or was she one of those women who was thrilled over the idea of being bitten by a vampire? It sickened him to think such thoughts.

She was texting on her phone when they got back to the table and she quickly put it away when she saw them. Brandt wondered who she'd been talking to. Did she have a boyfriend? Surely if she did, he wouldn't have let her come out tonight alone.

He placed her drink on the table and took a seat next to her, with Nolen claiming the chair on her other side. She seemed a little nervous sandwiched between them, but Brandt didn't want to back off. If she was in Luna del Morte, she obviously knew about werewolves, vampires, shapeshifters, and the other supernatural beings in the club. But he still wasn't sure how to tell her she was his mate, much less that she was the mate to both him *and* his brother.

"So what brings you to Luna del Morte tonight?" Nolen asked her, having to seemingly read Brandt's mind.

"My friends were talking about it, and… well, I just thought that maybe…" She stopped and played with the stem of her glass.

"Maybe what?" Brandt asked.

"I haven't had a lot of luck with men. I thought maybe I'd have better luck here."

Nolen ran his fingers through her hair and Brandt placed a hand on her thigh. She looked back and forth between them before settling her gaze on Brandt.

"I find it hard to believe that someone as beautiful as you has a difficult time finding men," he told her.

She blushed. "I'm not beautiful, I'm fat."

He growled. "Never say that again."

She bit her lip, drawing his attention to her plump, ripe mouth. He wanted to lean forward and kiss her, but he was afraid he'd scare her away if he did that. Instead, he leaned closer, pressing his shoulder against hers.

"You really came over here because you thought I was beautiful?" she asked.

Brandt nodded. "We both did."

"And in case you weren't sure," Nolen said, "we aren't human."

"Would it be out of line for me to ask what you are?" she asked.

Nolen grinned. "We're werewolves."

She seemed to digest that information before asking her next question. "If you're werewolves, shouldn't you be looking for your mates instead of going to clubs?"

"I came here specifically to find my mate," Brandt said.

"Then what are you doing wasting time with me?" she asked.

Nolen and Brandt shared a look. Now was the time. Did they tell her, or wait? And if they waited, would she be angry with them later for having withheld important information from her? It was tantamount to lying to her, lying by omission anyway, and they'd always prided themselves on telling the truth. Maybe they should have discussed this part while they were at the bar, the "what happens when she walks away" part.

"You're my mate," Brandt told her, watching as her eyes widened.

"And mine," Nolen said.

Her mouth opened and closed several times before snapping shut. It seemed they'd made her speechless. Brandt wasn't sure if that was a good sign or a bad one.

"I… Are you sure?" she asked.

Brandt nodded. "Positive."

"Maybe we should go somewhere else for this conversation," Nolen suggested

Brandt and Nolen stood, helping Falan to her feet. The trio made their way out of the club and onto the sidewalk out front. Once there, Brandt wasn't quite sure what to do. He'd love to tuck her into his truck and carry her to his house, but he wasn't sure she'd go for it. She might be his mate, but they were still strangers.

"What happens now?" Falan asked.

"We need to go somewhere quiet, someplace where we can talk," Nolen said. "I know we just met, but our house really would be the best place to go."

She shook her head. "No, but we can go to my house. I rent a small cottage from the Leicester family."

Brandt's eyebrows rose. The Leicesters were one of the richest families in Moonspell. Nowhere near as rich as Aidan Grant and his nest of vampires, but still rather wealthy.

"You're traveling in mighty lofty circles."

"My mom worked for them until she passed away. They let me have the place for a song so I can't complain, and I never have to worry about being evicted."

"We'll follow you," Nolen said.

Falan nodded and started walking to her car. Once Brandt and Nolen made sure she was safely ensconced in the vehicle, they headed to their truck. It was only a ten minute drive to her home. They followed her down the winding driveway, behind the main house and around to her cottage. It was a quaint white clapboard structure with a small porch and black shutters. Azalea bushes lined the front of the home, adding cheer to it with their bright pink blossoms.

Looking at her cozy house, Brandt hoped she would be happy in their home. Their house was rather plain. Gray with white trim, nary a shrub or flower in sight. But perhaps what the place really needed was a woman's touch. Maybe if Falan came to live with them, *when* Falan came to live with them, she could spruce the place up a bit.

They followed her to the door and into the house. She turned on a lamp on a table near the front window and motioned for them to have a seat.

"Make yourselves comfortable," she said. "Do you want anything to drink? I have coffee or soda."

Brandt shook his head. "I'm fine, but thanks."

"Same here," Nolen said.

Falan curled up in the chair beside the sofa, facing them, her legs tucked underneath her. Brandt would have thought her to be at ease around them, if it weren't for the slight tremble in her hands. Or perhaps it wasn't them so much as their news. Finding out you're mated to a werewolf was a rather serious matter, life changing. Just because they'd found her didn't mean they'd get to keep her. She could very well send them packing and say she never wanted to see them again.

"What do you know about werewolves?" Nolen asked.

She shrugged. "Not much. I know you can shift into a wolf at will, mate for life, and follow pack law."

"That's the basics, and all you really need to know at this point. It's the mating for life part that we need to discuss," Brandt said. "I know it's a lot to take in, but you really are our mate."

"How can I be the mate to both of you? Shouldn't you each have one of your own?"

Nolen nodded. "That's typically how it works, but I've heard of other cases like ours. It doesn't happen often, I don't think. It hasn't happened at all in our pack, not in this generation anyway. I don't know about during our grandfather's or great-grandfather's time."

"So what happens now?" she asked.

Brandt leaned forward, resting his arms on his knees. "Since you're human and unused to our ways, we can take things slowly if you'd like."

She looked from him to Nolen and back again. "But that's not what you want?"

Brandt shrugged. "We'd like to move forward as quickly as possible, now that we've found you."

Falan pushed her hair behind her ear with a shaky hand. "I don't think I'm ready for that yet. Could we… Could I just get to know you first? Maybe go out with you one at a time?"

Brandt and Nolen shared a look. If she wanted to start out seeing them separately, it would be hard to get her to see them together later. They needed to start as they meant to go on. But how to convince her of that? It was obvious they made her nervous, and he couldn't really blame her. She seemed unused to male attention and now she had both him and his brother focused on her. It would be enough to fluster any woman.

"Falan…"

"What if you spent a little time with each of us, but any dates involved all three of us?" Nolen asked, cutting off Brandt.

Falan looked a little uncertain.

"Maybe we should give you some time to process everything," Brandt said. "We'll leave our numbers for you, and when you're ready you can call us."

She twisted her hands in her lap. "Are you sure there hasn't been some mistake?"

"Mistake? No, there's no mistake," Nolen assured her. "We understand that a ménage relationship probably isn't what you wanted, but…"

"It isn't that. I mean, I've never contemplated one before, but I don't think it will be a problem."

Brandt frowned. "Then what exactly *is* the problem?"

"Well… Look at the two of you! You look like underwear models." She motioned to her body. "And there's me. Lots of me."

Brandt growled. "Don't! Don't even say you're fat."

"What else would you call it?" she shot back. "I'm barely five feet tall and I wear a size twenty! I can't put on a pair of jeans without oozing out the top of them."

Brandt reached and took her hand. "Baby, it just means there's more for us to love. We aren't exactly small men; we'd break a tiny woman."

She gave him a hopeful look. "You really mean it?"

"Of course he does." Nolen grinned. "The moment we saw you we both wanted to go dance with you."

"Yes, but that's only because I'm your mate."

Brandt shook his head. "We didn't know you were our mate until we had you on the dance floor. Before that we wanted you because you're sexy as hell."

His gaze caressed her body. "Just the thought of all those soft curves pressed against me makes me want to drag you off to the bedroom, or bend you over the sofa."

Her eyes widened and her tongue darted out to wet her lips. Brandt watched the motion, his hunger for her growing. Unable to fight his desires any longer, he leaned forward and captured her lips with his, stroking them softly, teasing them apart so he could slip inside for a taste. The tang of her strawberry margarita lingered on her tongue, but beyond that was her own sweet flavor.

She kissed him back tentatively, as if she'd never kissed a man before. But if anything, her untutored kiss made him want her even more. His beast was rising to the surface, clamoring to claim his mate. He'd never wanted anyone with the intensity he felt toward Falan. Not wanting to scare her, he began to pull back.

Brandt caressed her cheek and she leaned into his touch. It gave him hope that she wouldn't make them wait long to claim her. It wasn't that they couldn't wait. They weren't a couple of slavering dogs without any control over their baser urges. But the need to claim Falan was strong. Brandt knew he'd feel restless until she was in their home and in their bed.

Nolen pulled a business card from his wallet. Picking up a pen from the coffee table, he wrote something on the back and handed it to Falan. She pulled her hand from Brandt's to accept it.

"That has both of our cell phone numbers on it," Nolen said. "You can call us at any time of day."

She nodded.

"We're going to go, but I want you to lock up behind us," Brandt told her. "We'll give you space for a few days to think things through."

Falan followed them to the door. "I promise to call."

Brandt and Nolen stepped outside. They waited until they heard the locks engage before walking out into the night. Things might not have ended quite the way they wanted, but Brandt had every confidence they would hear from her soon.

Chapter Two

Falan curled up in her living room chair and touched her fingers to her lips. She'd read countless romance novels, but none of them had prepared her for Brandt's kiss. He'd taken her by surprise. The moment his lips had touched hers time stood still. They'd felt soft yet firm as they'd moved against hers. A shiver raked her body as she remembered his tongue slowly sliding into her mouth, then retreating only to return again. He'd tasted of beer, which she usually hated, but on Brandt it had been divine. She couldn't have asked for a better first kiss.

But why hadn't Nolen kissed her? He claimed she was his mate, too. Did he not want her as much as Brandt did? Or had he worried about overwhelming her? If only she'd had the courage to kiss him on his way out the door. Would his kiss affect her as strongly as Brandt's had?

She remembered how angry Brandt had seemed when she'd commented on her weight. She'd be the first to admit she had issues with her body.

She'd been teased mercilessly most of her life, and had watched as all of the guys she'd liked ignored her and went out with skinny girls. What message was she supposed to derive from that except that she was fat? Her dating experience certainly hadn't changed once she'd reached adulthood. Brandt was the first man -- no, make that the first *person* -- who'd ever called her sexy. It had made her feel all warm inside.

She understood what it meant to be their mate. And if she were honest with herself, she'd admit that she was thrilled. The thought of belonging, of being part of something special… it was all she'd ever wanted. She'd wished on countless stars to be sent a man to love who would love her in return, and now she'd been sent not one but two. She wasn't entirely certain she could satisfy one man, much less two. But the brothers didn't seem worried about it.

The thought of being intimate with Brandt and Nolen was both exciting and a little bit scary. She knew she couldn't expect real life to be anything like a romance novel, but she had to wonder if they would be slow and tender, like the hero in the book she'd been reading last night. Or would it be fast and hard and leave her breathless? No matter how they made love to her, she knew she had to be honest with them and tell them she was a virgin. It was the right thing to do.

She had no doubt that they'd each been with their fair share of women, but she wondered if they'd ever shared one before. Being their mate made her special, but she wanted to be special in other ways, too. It didn't see fair that they got to be her first kiss, first intimate caress, first and only in her bed, if she didn't get to be a first anything for them.

Falan had no doubt they'd be honest with her if she asked them about their sex lives; she just wasn't one hundred percent sure she wanted to hear their answers. Men who looked like Brandt and Nolen were far from celibate. She knew they were experienced; she just had to decide whether or not she wanted to know *how* experienced they were. Did she really want to hear about the other women in their lives?

She picked up the card on the table and looked at it. *Fitzgerald Renovations.* It seemed her two hunky guys were good with their hands. She blushed at the thought of what else those hands might be good at and put the card back on the table. Looking across the room at the phone, she wondered if she should call them. They'd said she could have a few days to think things over, but what was there to contemplate? She was destined to be with them, right? From what little she knew about werewolves, she knew she'd never have to worry about infidelity, or at least she thought she didn't. When a werewolf mated, it was for a life, or so she'd been told. The moment they realized she was their mate, they wouldn't see anyone but her. At least, that's how she understood it. She'd only known one werewolf before and the woman didn't live in Moonspell any longer. She'd found her mate in another pack two towns over. She and Stella hadn't discussed the pack much, but they'd talked about guys more than once.

Maybe it would be a good idea to give Stella a call. They didn't talk often anymore, but the werewolf had made sure to leave her new number with Falan when she'd moved.

She walked across the room and picked up the cordless phone. Dialing the number, she put the phone to her ear and went back to her chair. She curled up and waited, hoping her friend would answer. Finally, on the sixth ring, Stella picked up.

"Falan?"

"Hi, Stella. I hope I'm not calling too late."

"No, not at all. Everything okay?"

"Sort of. I had some questions for you."

"What kind of questions?" Stella asked.

"Werewolf questions."

There was a pause, then, "Why do you need to know about werewolves?"

"Because Brandt and Nolen Fitzgerald informed me I'm their mate."

Stella squealed. "That's wonderful!"

"Is it?"

"Do you know how many women have wanted to tame those two? It's past time for them to settle down."

"But, why me? Wouldn't they be better suited to another werewolf?"

"Honey, we don't pick our mates. They're chosen for us. If you were selected as their mate, then the three of you were destined to be together."

"You aren't shocked that they have to share me?"

Stella laughed. "I doubt yours will be the first ménage relationship the pack has had."

"What about…"

"What's really bothering you?"

"They're so much more experienced than I am. What if they're disappointed? I know you told me that werewolves mate for life, but what if I can't satisfy them? It would kill me if they went to another woman."

"Oh, honey, you won't have to worry about that, not with those two. There's no one more loyal than Brandt and Nolen. If you open yourself up to them and jump in with both feet, you won't regret it."

"You really think so?"

"I know so. Now, why don't you give them a call and tell them you're ready to discuss your relationship?"

"I don't know, Stella. Maybe I should take things slowly. You know, go on a few dates and get to know them."

Stella sighed. "It sounds like you've already make up your mind. Just remember that they'll be willing to do anything for you. As of today, you're their world."

"No pressure or anything."

They made their goodbyes and Falan hung up the phone. She set it down on the table and stood. Not remembering whether or not she'd locked her car, she grabbed her keys and stepped outside. Her foot landed in something warm and wet and down she went. When she saw the substance was blood, she screamed and scrambled to her feet. She turned to go back in the house and froze. *He's mine* was written in blood on the front of her home next to the door.

Heart pounding, she dashed inside, slammed the door shut and locked it. Since she'd never really dated, "he" could only be Brandt or Nolen. With shaky hands, she picked up the phone and dialed both their numbers. Nolen didn't answer so she left a message, but Brandt answered almost immediately.

"Hello, beautiful. I didn't expect to hear from you for at least a day or two."

"Brandt, I... I need you." She couldn't hide the tremor in her voice.

"What's wrong, baby?"

"There's blood. So much blood. I don't know what to do."

"Falan, don't move. I'm on my way."

She disconnected the call and looked down at herself. She was covered in blood. Fighting back a sob, she practically ran down the hall to her bedroom. Going straight to her bathroom, she stripped out of her clothes and got in the shower. Scrubbing her skin, she watched as the blood washed down the drain. When she felt clean, she shut off the water and got out. She'd just wrapped a fluffy towel around her body when she heard a knock at the door.

Falan made her way to the front door and paused just before opening it. She peered through the peephole and sighed in relief when she saw it was Brandt. Quickly unlocking the door, she opened it to let him in. She noticed he was careful to step over the blood, not that she hadn't already tracked some inside.

Brandt closed the door and immediately gathered her in his arms. She wrapped her arms around his waist and breathed in his scent. Just knowing she wasn't alone made her feel better.

"Are you okay?" he asked.

She nodded. "Just a little scared. I wouldn't have called, but I didn't know what else to do."

"You did the right thing. Why don't you go put some clothes on and we'll get the police out here? They'll need to document this."

A tremor raked her body. "Do we have to call them?"

"The other option is to call my alpha, but someone with authority needs to know about this."

"I don't understand why it happened. It isn't like we've been seen together before now."

"Maybe someone heard me say you're our mate. There's no way to know which one of us they meant."

"Were either of you seeing someone seriously?" she asked.

"No. We dated casually, usually no more than three dates per woman. I know that doesn't put us in a favorable light, but we knew none of them was a mate for either of us."

She nodded. She'd known they'd been with other women. Men who looked like them would have their pick. The psycho who'd left the little present outside could be anyone. How were they going to keep it from happening again when they didn't know who'd made the threat?

"I don't know who to call. If a human did this, your alpha won't be able to do anything."

"Then we'll call the police."

Falan nodded again and moved away from him. She walked down the hall to her bedroom and pushed the door closed. Getting out her T-shirt and sleep pants, she got dressed. It wasn't sexy by any means, but she'd be sufficiently covered when the police arrived and she'd be comfortable.

She went into the bathroom, brushed her hair and braided it. Feeling a little bit better, she went in search of Brandt. She found him in the living room with his cell phone held to his ear.

He frowned and hung up the phone. "I can't reach Nolen. That's the second time I've tried."

"I called him, too."

"He probably can't hear over all the noise."

"Noise?"

"He was too keyed up to sleep so he went dancing."

At her stricken look, he rushed to assure her, "It's just dancing. He would've preferred to take you, but we'd just told you we'd give you some space. I promise he won't do anything that would hurt you."

"Why didn't you go with him?"

"I was content to stay home. Nolen is more in to partying than I am."

"I'm afraid I'm more the type to stay home. What happens when he wants to go out and I want to stay in?" She gave him a worried look. "I don't think this is going to work."

Brandt took her hand and led her over to the sofa. Pulling her down into his lap, he cuddled her close. She leaned into him, enjoying his arms around her.

"It's going to work. We'll discuss your concerns with Nolen and work through it. Maybe you can compromise and go to a club with him once a week."

"Maybe, if you think he'd really go for something like that."

"For now, let's focus on the problem at hand. I think we should take the threat seriously."

"Do you really think the police can help?"

"I don't know, but I'll feel better if they're keeping an eye on you."

"Thank you for coming. I don't think I could've faced this alone."

He caressed her cheek. "I'm glad you called me."

It took the police another fifteen minutes to show up and nearly an hour to take her statement and take pictures. Once they were gone, Brandt went outside to clean up the mess. Falan curled up on the sofa and waited for him to finish.

She couldn't imagine what she'd have done if she'd have been alone to face this. Having Brandt by her side kept her steady. She only wished Nolen would call or come by. The only thing better than having one Fitzgerald brother by her side would be having both of them with her.

Brandt came in and locked the door. She didn't know how he'd managed it, but there wasn't a drop of blood on him. She patted the cushion beside her in hopes he'd come sit with her. While she was holding up fairly well, she needed his strength.

He walked toward her and knelt at her feet. He took her hand in his and rubbed his thumb across her knuckles.

"I should probably go," he said. "It's pretty late."

"I don't want to be alone tonight."

"What are you saying, Falan?"

"Would you... would you stay with me?"

He cupped her cheek with his other hand. "Are you sure?"

"I'm positive. I need you."

"Then I'll stay."

Brandt stood and helped her to her feet. With an arm around her waist, he guided her to the bedroom. He pulled back the blankets and helped her into bed. When he turned to leave, she stopped him.

"Stay."

He paused. "I don't know that that's such a good idea."

"Please, Brandt."

He closed the bedroom door and began removing his clothes. Falan drank in the sight of him. He was so strong, his muscles well-defined. Her mouth watered as he stripped down to his underwear. A blush heated her cheeks when she saw the bulge between his legs. Now she understood why he'd wanted to sleep elsewhere. It seemed that despite their rather horrific night, he wanted her.

Brandt walked around the bed and slipped under the covers. He reached for her and pulled her into his arms. She rested her head on his chest and listened to his heart beating under her ear. She already felt better.

As she relaxed against him, she closed her eyes. Being in Brandt's arms made her feel safe and cared for, but she wished Nolen had come with him. If being with one Fitzgerald brother felt his good, she could only imagine how wonderful it would feel to lie between them.

Chapter Three

Morning sun filtered through the window and Brandt slowly came awake. The first thing he noticed was the soft, warm body pressed against him. He cuddled Falan close, loving the feel of her in his arms. The morning was nearly perfect. The only thing missing was Nolen.

He worried about his brother. As soon as he got the message that Falan needed them, he should have come running. Not only had they not seen Nolen last night, they hadn't heard from him either. What could have possibly kept him? He knew his brother well enough to know it wasn't another woman.

Falan stirred beside him and snuggled closer, throwing her leg over one of his. He felt his cock harden and bit back a groan. He would love nothing more than to claim her, but this wasn't the right moment. Nolen should be with them the first time.

Brandt tightened his arms around his mate and kissed the top of her head. They'd just met, but she was already precious to him. He'd gladly lay down his life for her, if it came to that.

She stretched and opened her eyes. Looking bashful, she smiled up at him.

"Morning," he said.

"Good morning."

"I'd ask how you slept, but I don't think you even moved until this morning."

She blushed. "I can't remember a time I've slept so well."

"Me neither."

He lowered his head to kiss her, his mouth devouring hers as he gave her a passionate, toe curling kiss. His lips drank from hers hungrily, until they were interrupted by a knock at the door. Brandt pulled back and smoothed her hair away from her face.

"I'll go see who that is," he told her.

"I'll come with you."

They got out of bed and made their way to the front door. Whoever was on the other side pounded on it again. Brandt moved in front of Falan and opened the door, not caring that he only wore his boxer briefs.

"Well, I see now why I didn't get any more calls last night," Nolen said as he shouldered his way past his brother.

"Where the hell have you been?" Brandt asked as he closed the door.

"I had a little too much to drink last night and Oran drove me to his place. I didn't see the missed calls and messages until this morning. I tried to call your cell, but it went straight to voicemail."

"It must have died last night."

Falan moved closer to Nolen and reached for him. Brandt watched the indecision on Nolen's face and his hesitancy as he held out a hand to their mate. His brother seemed tense and he didn't know why. It was obvious that their mate was fine, so that couldn't be it. But even as Nolen pulled her to his side, he seemed stiff.

"You're not single anymore, Nolen. You can't go entire nights without checking your phone," Brandt told him. "Our mate needed us."

"She had you."

Falan looked up at Nolen. "I wanted both of you here."

His jaw tightened. "You seem to have done all right with just one of us."

Falan looked hurt by his brother's behavior and Brandt didn't know what to do. Nolen had never acted like this before. If he didn't know better, he would say his brother was jealous. But that was absurd! They shared Falan equally, as she was mate to both of them. Surely his brother understood that. He couldn't possibly think… Brandt looked down at his state of undress and back at his brother.

"What exactly is going through your head, little brother?"

Nolen growled. "I hate it when you call me that! I'm only younger by two minutes."

"Answer the question."

"I think that you claimed her last night."

Falan gasped and moved away from Nolen.

"Do you honestly think I would leave you out of something important like that?" Brandt asked. "It would be different if we'd already claimed her, but our first time with her should be together."

"You obviously stayed the night."

"Yeah, dumbass, and if you'd answered your damn phone you would have, too. She wanted both of us here. Some whack job poured blood all over her porch and wrote 'he's mine' in blood by her front door. She needed us and you were off partying somewhere."

Nolen looked chagrined. "I was celebrating. I didn't think to check my phone. I've never had to before."

"We have the responsibility of a mate now. It's time to grow up and act your age."

Nolen nodded. "Or maybe I should just…"

Brandt narrowed his eyes. "You should just what?"

"Maybe I should give the two of you time to get to know one another better. Once she's used to the ways of our kind, then I can come back."

"No!" Falan placed her hand on his arm. "Please, don't shut me out."

"I'll help track down the person responsible for last night's events," Nolen told her. "But other than that…"

"Nolen, please. Whatever I've done…"

He silenced Falan. "It isn't you, sweetheart. It's me. I'm no good for you."

"Don't say that. You and Brandt, I've never had such good fortune before. And last night, when I was lying in bed, all I could think about was how wonderful it would be if both of you were here. I wanted to be surrounded by you, to know that I was safe and cared for. No matter what you say, I know you can give me that."

Nolen shared a look with Brandt before looking down at Falan again. "You truly wish me to stay?"

She nodded.

"I'll stay on one condition."

"Anything," she said. Brandt noticed the hope shining her eyes.

"If something happens between us, if you should find yourself alone with either myself or Brandt, and you wish to be intimate, you won't wait for the other to join you. I know you want all three of us to be present the first time, but I'd rather let nature take its course."

She looked surprised, and honestly, Brandt was too. He'd thought his brother would want to share. It wasn't the first time they'd shared a woman, and now that they were both mated to Falan, it wouldn't be the last.

"If that's what you want," she said softly. It was obvious to Brandt that she'd hoped for more from Nolen, but for whatever reason his brother was holding back.

"It isn't that I don't want you, Falan, far from it. I just don't want to force the relationship. I don't want you to feel pressured to be with both of us. Something tells me that's not something you've done before."

She blushed and Brandt knew his brother was right, but then he'd suspected as much already. But just because she was new to that way of life didn't mean she couldn't handle it. Maybe Nolen wasn't giving her enough credit. Perhaps they needed to embrace their relationship instead of sheltering Falan from it. Or was there something more going on? Was Nolen the one not ready to face their new life?

"What are the police doing about last night's events?" Nolen asked.

"Not much of anything. They said they'd keep an eye on the place, but we know what that means."

"Yeah. We need to get Hayden over here," Nolen said. "Did you ask for copies of the pictures?"

"I snapped a few with my phone. It was the best I could do."

Nolen pulled out his cell phone. "I'll get Hayden over here so we can figure out what to do next."

Brandt glanced at the clock on the wall. "Are you sure that's a good idea? It's barely seven."

"Maybe you're right. I'm not worried about waking up Hayden, but if the phone wakes Daniela…"

"Who's Daniela?" Falan asked.

"Our alpha's mate. They met when Daniela was kidnapped by the local vampire nest. It's leader, Aidan Grant, wanted to make her his bride."

"And your alpha objected."

Brandt grinned. "Most definitely. Daniela is his whole world. On top of that, she's carrying their first child. She was pregnant when Aidan took her from our alpha. But Daniela is brave and resourceful. She managed to escape and made her way to Hayden's side. I'm still not sure what happened, but somehow, they convinced the vampires to leave Daniela alone. Aidan left that night with another woman, Serenity, a friend of the pack. Our alpha said it was her idea and we have no reason not to believe him."

"I wish I could be like that," Falan said wistfully.

"Like what?" Nolen asked.

"Brave and strong. I've spent most of my life hearing how ugly, stupid, and fat I am that after a while I started to believe it. It got so bad that for the longest time I couldn't even look in the mirror."

Nolen lifted her chin so they were looking into one another's eyes. "And now?"

"It's better, but… I don't need a mirror or another person to tell me I'm fat. If I were six inches taller, being a size twenty wouldn't be so bad. But I'm barely five feet tall. I passed pudgy a few sizes ago."

Nolen ran his hands down her body and pulled her close. "Sweetheart, you may be more than a handful, but I never want to hear you call yourself fat ever again. If you want to lose weight, we'll respect that. But don't lose weight to please anyone other than yourself because we happen to love your body just the way it is."

There was a look of wonder on her face. "You really mean that?"

Brandt moved in behind her and placed his hands on her hips, caging her in between them. "Of course he means it, baby. You're the sexiest, most beautiful woman we've ever seen and we wouldn't change a thing about you."

Nolen lowered his head and slanted his mouth across hers, kissing her deeply and passionately. Not wanting to be left out, Brandt trailed slow kisses down her neck. When he reached her shoulder, he nosed her shirt aside and gently bit and sucked her soft skin, leaving his mark on her. Nolen lifted his head and their mate clung to him.

"Please," she said softly. "I want you. Both of you."

Brandt and Nolen shared a look and Nolen nodded. They herded her down the hall to the bedroom and gently closed the door.

She trembled slightly. "I've never…"

"We know, baby. We figured you hadn't been with two men before."

She shook her head. "That wasn't what I was going to say."

Brandt growled. "Who were they?"

"Who were… Oh! No, no I've never… That is, I… I've never been with *one* man, much less two."

Nolen crossed to her side. "Sweetheart, are you trying to tell us you're a virgin?"

She blushed and nodded.

Brandt felt his anger drain away and moved to take her in his arms. Holding her close, he breathed in her scent. She was not only theirs, but she'd never belonged to anyone else. His wolf wanted to howl and urged him to claim her, but he refused to give in to his baser urges.

"What do you need from us?" he asked her. "The last thing we want to do is scare you."

"Neither of you scares me. I just don't quite know what to expect. I've read romance novels before, but they're just fiction. Surely it doesn't happen quite like that."

"Like what?" Nolen asked.

"So perfectly."

"Well, I don't know that there's such a thing as perfect sex, but we can certainly get pretty damn close," Brandt told her.

She frowned. "I guess you've both been with lots of women."

Nolen silenced her. "Think of it as practice for this moment, so we'd know exactly what you need from us."

"Then why ask me?"

"Because we don't want to move too fast," Brandt said. "We both want you desperately, but we're trying to hold back."

She placed her hands on his chest. "What if I don't want you to hold back?"

"Baby, we don't want to hurt you, and your first time should be special."

"It is special. It's with you and Nolen."

Brandt looked at Nolen. "Do you have any condoms? I think I've got one in my wallet, but I get the feeling that won't be enough."

"You know I always have a stash in my truck."

Falan looked over her shoulder at him and he shrugged. "It was just the way I lived my life before we met you yesterday. I promise you'll never have to worry that I'm with another woman. You're the only one I want."

She looked up at Brandt. "And you?"

"The moment I saw you across the club last night I knew I wanted to dance with you. There was something about you that called to me; I just didn't know what it was. And once I found out you were my mate, you owned me completely. There will never be a woman out there who could ever compare to you."

He saw the sheen of tears in her eyes as he caressed her cheek with the back of his fingers. "Do you not realize how precious you are to us?" He lowered his head and kissed her gently. "You mean everything to us, baby."

"Make love to me. Both of you. I want you to show me what I've been missing."

"Just as soon as Nolen goes to the truck."

They'd always used condoms, and while Brandt knew that being with their mate would be different, he somehow doubted she wanted to start a family right away. Besides, she hardly knew them. Even though they were both clean, that didn't mean she would want to be with them without barriers. Someday, but not today.

"Why don't you take a hot, relaxing shower? We'll come get you in a few minutes," Brandt said.

She nodded and went into the adjoining bathroom. After he heard the water turn on, Brandt turn to Nolen.

"Do you want to join her in the shower or gather some candles to make this room a little more romantic?"

"I'll take the room. I think she feels more comfortable around you right now."

Brandt nodded before stripping out of his clothes and joining Falan in the bathroom.

* * *

Brandt took a moment to enjoy the view. Falan's shower was rather large and enclosed on two sides by glass. She was rinsing the shampoo from her hair with her head tipped back and her eyes closed.

Quietly opening the shower, he stepped inside and closed the door. Falan blinked the water from her eyes and shrieked when she saw him. Her cheeks turned a becoming shade of pink.

"What are you doing in here?" she asked.

"I thought I'd help you wash."

Her cheeks burned even brighter. "I'm sure I can manage."

Brandt gathered her in his arms and pulled her close. His cock was hard and throbbing between them. Words couldn't describe how wonderful she felt against him.

"Why are you here? I mean, why are you really here?"

"Here in your shower or in your home?"

"The shower."

"Because I want to be. Can you not tell how much I want you?"

Her eyes flicked down and back up. "I think I have an idea."

He grinned. Tangling his hand in her long hair, he tilted her head back. His mouth devoured hers hungrily, tasting, teasing, claiming. He wanted there to be little doubt in her mind that she was belonged to him. Never had he wanted a woman as much as he wanted Falan.

When the kiss ended, she touched her swollen lips and smiled up at him. "Would it be wrong of me to ask you to kiss me again?"

"No, but kissing leads to other things, and I'm not about to take your virginity in the shower."

That sobered her. "Brandt, I want you to be the one."

"The one what?"

"Who takes my virginity."

"Baby…"

"No, I can tell Nolen isn't into this wholeheartedly. I want to be with him, but I don't want him to be my first. You've been by my side since the moment I said I needed you, and I can tell you have no doubts about starting a relationship with me."

"Starting… Baby, the moment I knew you were mine we were in a committed relationship. There's no starting to it."

"Why doesn't Nolen feel the same way?"

"He does. He just…" He sighed. "I'm honestly not sure what's going through his head right now. He wanted to take a step back from the relationship, but I think he's worked things out in his head now."

"He doesn't want me?"

"It isn't that. Don't ever think that. He's just always been a party guy. I think being in a committed relationship makes him a little uneasy."

"But you want me?"

He hesitated a moment. "I wanted a mate when we found you, same as Nolen, but I don't think he thought about how much it would change his life. I'm ready to embrace whatever changes you bring to my life."

"I want to start a life with you," he told her. "I'm ready to jump into this relationship with both feet."

Brandt soaped his hands and began to gently soap her skin. When he reached her breasts, he cupped them and stroked her nipples with his thumbs. Her eyes slid shut and she bit her lip as she arched her back. Her nipples hardened under his touch. He tweaked the distended tips drawing a gasp from her sweet lips.

After lavishing attention on the bountiful mounds, his hands moved lower, sliding down her belly to her pussy. He was more than a little surprised to see it was trimmed. His questing fingers delved between the lips of her pussy, stroking the satiny skin until he found her clit. He caressed the bundle of nerves, his fingers sliding across the nub in tormenting circles.

Falan's hands grabbed his arms and held on. He cupped one of her breasts in one hand and played with her nipple while he teased her clit. He felt her body tense a moment before she came. Even in the shower, he could smell her juices as they trickled down her legs.

"Brandt, I never…"

He looked surprised. "You've never had an orgasm? Not by your own hand or a toy?"

She blushed. "I've never used a vibrator or anything, and I've never been able to make myself come."

"Let's get you cleaned up and see what Nolen's been up to."

Brandt quickly washed her and himself. After rinsing, he turned off the water and dried off Falan, then himself. He opened the bedroom door and was pleasantly surprised. Nolen had found flowers somewhere and strewn the petals across the floor. The sheets were pulled down and candles covered the bedside table and dresser. He'd closed the blinds to keep out any prying eyes.

* * *

Falan faced Nolen, feeling uncertain. He didn't seem committed to her, and yet he'd shown a romantic side by preparing the bedroom. Had he had a change of heart? Brandt had said he thought Nolen had worked through his issues. She could only hope that was true. She wanted their relationship to work.

Nolen, having undressed while they were in the shower, stood before her in all his naked glory. He came to stand before her and caressed her cheek. She tried to read his expression, but had no idea what he was thinking.

"I heard what you said," he told her. "And you're right. I haven't been as committed as I should've been. I wanted you, but I wanted it to be on my terms. That was wrong of me and I'm sorry."

"What are you saying, Nolen?"

"I'm saying that I may feel things differently than Brandt does, and I may not react the way you want me to, but I want you to know that I do care about you and I'm looking forward to sharing my life with you."

Falan pulled him closer and kissed him. She felt Brandt behind her, placing his hands on her hips and trailing kisses down her neck and across her shoulders. Nolen gently gripped her arms, holding her to him. When he pulled back, her heart was pounding.

Brandt herded them toward the bed, then lifted her and laid her on the mattress. She looked up at him in wide-eyed wonder, amazed that he'd lifted her with such ease. He'd managed what no other man had before -- he'd made her feel small and delicate. She reached for him, tugging him onto the bed, then crooked her finger at Nolen. With her men on either side of her, her body warmed in anticipation. In theory, she knew what happened next, at least, with one man and woman. She was starting to wish she'd read a ménage romance or two. Maybe then she'd be better prepared for this moment.

Nolen nuzzled her neck and cupped one breast. While Brandt latched onto her other nipple, Nolen pinched and rolled her distended nipple; Brandt sucked the other and grazed it with his teeth. She felt liquid drip down her thighs and began to squirm.

Brandt's hand caressed her belly before slipping between her thighs. He delved between the lips of her pussy, spreading her juices over her clit. He circled and teased the nub until she was writhing under them. He brushed the sensitive area with his thumb and eased two fingers inside of her. Falan gasped and lifted her hips.

She felt hot, like every nerve burned and tingled. Her body was straining toward something, something just out of reach. Nolen claimed her lips while Brandt's fingers pumped in and out of her. She felt her body tightening just like it had in the shower, and then she was tumbling over the edge.

Brandt slid his fingers from her body and sucked her juices from the digits. She was surprised to discover it turned her on. Nolen moved away from her to lean against the headboard, then he was reaching for her, pulling her back against his chest.

Brandt rolled on a condom then moved over her, spreading her legs. Settling between her thighs, he began easing his cock inside of her, stretching her. When he felt her hymen, he pushed through then stilled, giving her time to adjust. Nolen murmured softly in her ear, telling her how beautiful and sexy she was, how lucky they were to have her. When Brandt began moving inside of her, she found that it didn't hurt. As he entered her over and over again, she lifted her hips.

Nolen pinched and rolled her nipples as Brandt plunged into her harder and faster. Her body began to burn and as Brandt thrust into her one last time she came. Nolen kissed her next and stroked her body, bringing her down from her high.

She began to shift so she could sit up, but Nolen stopped her.

"Wait a minute, sweetheart. Let Brandt clean you up."

Sure enough, his brother slipped from her body and rose from the bed, returning a moment later with a warm wet rag. He wiped the blood from her thighs then returned to the bathroom.

"My turn now, sweetheart," Nolen said. "Unless you're too sore?"

She shook her head, but she wasn't sure she'd survive a fourth orgasm. Could she even have another one? Nolen turned and lifted her so she was straddling him. He quickly rolled a condom down his hard shaft and slowly, he lowered her onto his cock. She felt the bed dip and then Brandt's hands were on her hips.

"I'm going to help you move," Brandt said softly.

She tipped her head back and rested it on his chest, her hands splayed on Nolen's chest. She rocked her hips back and forth, loving the feel of Nolen's hard cock inside of her. Brandt helped her move, creating a delicious friction. Nolen cupped her breasts and played with her nipples. Feeling brave, she reached between her legs and fingered her sensitive clit.

Nolen grinned. "That's so hot!"

She bit her lip and worked her clit faster. Just when she thought she couldn't take any more, she went flying, soaring to heights she'd never dreamed of before. She felt her inner walls clench and release Nolen's cock, and then he was exploding inside of her.

She slumped over his chest, feeling spent, her limbs like jelly. Brandt and Nolen had surpassed her dreams. Being with them was wonderful.

She felt Brandt move away and a minute later he was back with a fresh rag in his hand. He lifted her from Nolen and cleaned her. When Nolen rose from the bed, Brandt tossed the cloth to him. Pulling Falan into his arms, he cuddled her close.

"Are you okay?" he asked.

"I'm wonderful."

He smiled and kissed her. "Now there can be no doubt you're ours."

She traced the intricate tattoo now covering his shoulder and upper arm. She'd noticed Nolen had one, too. They'd appeared as if by magic and she wondered about the significance of the marks.

"Where did this come from?" she asked.

"When a werewolf finds his mate and is intimate with her for the first time, he's marked. Now everyone will know we belong to you."

She smiled, delighted. Hearing him say they were hers, and that they'd been marked as such, made her heart sing.

"I'm surprised you didn't want to brand me."

"Brand, no. Tattoo… that's another matter."

She smacked him on the arm. "I'm *not* getting a tattoo."

He sighed. "It's a little late for that, baby. Not only is a werewolf marked when he finds his mate, but his mate is also marked. You now have a crescent moon in the middle of your back, showing you're ours."

"No one will ever see it," she said. "So marked or not, no one will know I belong to you."

Nolen rejoined them. "There's one other way."

"What's that?" Falan asked.

"Mom's ring."

Brandt laced his fingers with hers. "What do you say, baby? Will you wear our ring?"

Tears gathered in her eyes. "Yes. Yes, I'll wear your ring."

"We'll get it for you today. After breakfast we'll go home, but we'll come back and pick you up for dinner."

"We don't have to go out. I can make something here."

"Let us spoil you a little," Nolen said. "You might as well get used to it. Once you move in, you'll have us waiting on you hand and foot."

"Move in?" she asked. She supposed that was a logical conclusion, but things were moving a little too quickly. "No one said anything about me moving."

Brandt tugged her closer. "Baby, what did you expect us to do? Live apart from our mate and only visit you on occasion?"

"Honestly, I hadn't had time to really think about it. Everything is moving so fast. We just met and yet we've already slept together and now there's talk of me moving. I can't process all of this right now."

Brandt sighed and kissed the top of her head. "We have time. Nothing has to be done today. There's no reason we can't give you a few days. That had been our intention before you called last night."

"About that… Do you think it was a one time deal?" she asked.

"It's hard to say." Nolen frowned. "I don't like the idea of you being alone here at night. If she does come back, you should have someone with you. If you don't want both of us here at the same time, we could take turns staying the night."

She shook her head. "I can't rely on you to take care of me 24-7. There are going to be times when I'm alone. You should keep to your usual schedules."

Brandt snorted. "I'm not going near a club unless you're with me. And since that's normal for me, I think it's safe to say I'll be altering my life a bit."

"Same here, sweetheart. Last night showed me that I need to make some changes in my life."

"Whether you like it or not, you're stuck with us," Brandt said. "When we aren't working, we'll be stuck to you like glue."

She nodded. "All right. If that's really what you want, I won't fight you on it."

Nolen held his hand out to her. "Come on. Let's get dressed and grab some breakfast. Then we'll leave you in peace for a little while."

Falan let him help her out of bed. "If the two of you will excuse me, I'm just going to rinse off in the shower."

Nolen brushed a kiss against her cheek and gave her a gentle shove toward the bathroom. After she closed the door, she looked at her reflection. She was glowing; her eyes were bright. It seemed the Fitzgerald brothers were good for her.

With a smile, she started the shower. She stepped under the hot spray and closed her eyes. As she washed her body, she found herself humming happily. Her two wolves had put a smile on her face that would probably be present all day.

Chapter Four

Several hours later, Nolen pulled into Falan's driveway. The first thing he noticed was her car -- sitting on four flat tires. He got out of the truck and went to inspect the smaller vehicle. His good mood quickly turned to rage.

Without knocking, he entered Falan's home and called out her name.

"I'm in the bedroom."

He locked the door and walked down the hall to her bedroom. When he stepped into the room, he found Falan spritzing some perfume on her wrists. While the scent was pleasing, he should have told her that she smelled better than any perfume.

"When's the last time you went outside?" he asked as he leaned against the doorframe.

"I don't know. Around noon when I got the mail."

"Did you notice anything unusual about your car?"

She shook her head.

"Your tires have been slashed."

Her face paled. "There must be some mistake."

Nolen shook his head. "I'm afraid not, sweetheart."

"What should I do, Nolen? Call the police again?"

He grinned. "How is it you can tell us apart?"

"You're the one who calls me sweetheart, but I knew it was you before that. You carry yourself differently than Brandt does."

He pulled her into his arms. "We'll call the police. Once they've left, we'll go to dinner."

She looked surprised. "Brandt's not coming?"

"Last minute client meeting. We flipped a coin to see which of us would have the honor of your company."

At her insulted look, he rushed to assure her, "We both wanted to come. If it weren't for the coin toss, we would have fought."

"Well, I wouldn't have wanted that."

"Come on. Let's call the police so we can get on with our evening. I'll call Brandt and let him know what happened."

"Do you really think calling the police is going to fix anything? Someone hates me enough to slash my tires, Nolen. If the police had been doing their job, the psycho wouldn't have gotten close to my house again."

He tightened his arms around her. "They're doing the best they can, sweetheart. Brandt and I shouldn't have left you alone. We won't make that mistake again."

"You seem awfully calm."

"It's an illusion. I'm ready to disembowel someone. And when Brandt finds out she's been back, he'll be ready to kill someone, too. There's nothing more important to us than you."

"Are you sure you don't know who it is?" she asked. "It has to be a crazy ex-girlfriend."

He cleared his throat. "We, um… we don't have ex-girlfriends."

Falan snorted. "You can't expect me to believe you haven't dated."

"Casually, yes."

His words made her recall a similar discussion with Brandt. "So it was all about sex for both of you?"

He nodded. "Doesn't put us in a very favorable light, does it?"

"Just makes you a typical guy, I guess. From what I've seen of men, most forget to think with their brains when women are around."

Nolen winced. "For what it's worth, those days are behind me."

"This isn't getting us anywhere. Just call the police so we can move on with our evening. I'll have to call someone to replace the tires."

"Me and Brandt will take care of that. It's the least we can do. I know you still want your independence, but you have to understand our need to take care of you."

"Fine. You replace the tires."

He kissed her briefly before releasing her and reaching for his phone. He called the police and explained the situation to them. They assured them someone would be out momentarily. After that, it was a waiting game.

It took nearly half an hour for the officers to show up. They took Nolen's statement since he first noticed the tires, then took pictures for evidence. When they were finished, Nolen stepped outside to have a word with them.

"Look, we know you can't watch her house 24-7, but how did the crazy woman manage to slip past you?"

"Like you said, we can't watch the place all the time. Maybe your pack should help out. Have you even told your alpha what happened?" the lead officer asked.

"I think Brandt was supposed to, but I don't know if he ever did. I'll call Hayden and see what he thinks of this mess."

"See that you do. Chances are the problem is closer to home than you think."

Nolen frowned. Could they be right? Was it possible the woman responsible for terrorizing Falan was part of the pack? If that was the case, Hayden definitely needed to know what was going on. He wouldn't tolerate this kind of behavior.

He pulled out his phone and quickly dialed his alpha's number. At first, he didn't think anyone would answer. But after the seventh ring, the alpha's mate picked up.

"Hello."

"Daniela, this is Nolen Fitzgerald. I'm looking for Hayden."

"Just a minute, Nolen. He's putting a baby bed together."

Nolen grinned. He knew his alpha had waited a long time to find his mate and have children. It was all too easy to picture the big man in the floor screwing together a crib.

"Nolen, is this a social call or did you need something?" Hayden asked.

"Have you heard from Brandt lately?"

"No. I can't say that I have."

"We found our mate at Luna del Morte yesterday."

"We? You mean you have the same mate?" Hayden asked.

"Yeah. Unconventional, but not unheard of."

"So what can I do for you?"

"She's received two threats since meeting us. The police suggested it could be someone in the pack."

Hayden growled. "What kind of threats?"

"Someone wrote 'he's mine' in blood on her house last night and tonight her tires were slashed."

"And we know for sure they aren't talking about another man in her life?"

"There isn't one. She's never really dated before so they can only mean one of us. Problem is, we don't know which one."

"Give me her address and I'll assign someone to keep an eye on the place," Hayden said.

Nolen rattled off the address. "I'll let Falan know someone will be watching her place. It might make her feel better."

"If she's your mate, why doesn't she just move in with you?"

"She's not used to our ways yet. I don't want to rush her."

Hayden snorted. "Don't tell me you're mated to a fairy."

Nolen laughed. "No, she's not a fairy. Actually, she's a human. She seems to know a little about us so I'm guessing she's made friends with a werewolf somewhere along the way."

"A human? Daniela will be thrilled. The women in the pack have been welcoming, but I know she'd prefer the company of her own kind."

"Maybe the two of them can meet soon," Nolen suggested. If Falan made a friend in the pack, maybe she'd feel more content settling into her role as their mate. He knew she was still holding back, not quite ready to commit. He could feel it.

"I'll have Daniela drop by one day this week. I'm sure she'll take along a little welcome gift of some sort."

"I'd appreciate that. Anything to help Falan settle in with the pack and her new life."

"Go take care of your mate. I'm calling Seamus now to set up a guard rotation for Falan's house. We'll take care of her."

"Thanks, Hayden."

Nolen ended the call and quickly sent a text to his brother. He knew if Brandt showed up and saw the car he'd be worried first and then furious. He briefly let his twin know that Falan was safe and both the police and Hayden had been called. He shoved the phone back in his pocket and went back inside to find his mate. Despite the nonchalance he'd shown her in regard to the incident, he was inwardly shaking with fury. The thought that someone meant harm to his mate had him seething. But he needed to keep it together for Falan's sake. He knew she was scared and worried, and he didn't know how to take that fear away. She should be able to live in her home, her sanctuary, without fearing that someone would do her harm.

He found her sitting on the sofa, her face pinched. She looked like she'd shed a few tears while he'd been outside. Nolen knelt at her feet and gathered her hands in his. Bringing them to his lips, he kissed her knuckles.

"If you aren't up for dinner, we'll order in and spend the night watching movies," he told her.

"But you made plans for tonight."

"Plans can be changed. We can go out to dinner any time. If you don't feel up to it, we won't go tonight."

"I think I'd rather stay in."

He leaned forward and brushed his lips against hers. "Then we'll order in. Pick anything you want and I'll have someone pick it up for us."

"If we order Chinese, they'll deliver."

Nolen frowned. "The only Chinese place in town is Wang's over on Bloomfield, and I speak from experience when I say they don't deliver."

She smiled. "They may not deliver to a couple of womanizers like you and Brandt, but I assure you they'll deliver to me."

He winced at the reminder of his not so distant past. He was completely defenseless against her, knowing she spoke the truth. It was very likely Mr. and Mrs. Wang had refused to deliver to him based on his reputation. It certainly didn't help his cause that he'd hit on their only daughter in high school. They'd made it clear back then that he wasn't suitable.

"I guess that means you're placing the order," he said.

"That would probably be for the best."

"Then order me some sweet and sour chicken, fried rice, and egg rolls."

Her jaw dropped. "That's exactly what I order."

Nolen grinned. "Better make it two then."

She reached for her phone and quickly dialed the number. While she was placing their order, Nolen glanced out her front window through the blinds. Everything seemed quiet. He hoped there wouldn't be another incident tonight, or any night really. He wished they could find the culprit and put an end to it. It wasn't right that their woman should live in fear.

Falan hung up the phone and smiled at him. "They said it would be here in about thirty minutes. Did you want to pick out a movie? I don't own very many, but I have some in the entertainment center under the TV."

He knelt in front of the TV and slid open the doors on the entertainment center. She was right, she didn't own much. Quickly flipping through them, he saw a common theme – romance. He also noticed she liked dancing movies like *Footloose* and *Save the Last Dance*. Faced with the overly feminine selection, he wasn't sure what to choose. He pulled out several, trying to determine which looked the most worn so he could determine her favorite. He heard a *thunk* and leaned down to see what had fallen. Shoved to the back was a hidden set of DVDs. He pulled out the fallen one and smiled. *Supernatural* season one. So what if they didn't get everything right? It was still one of his favorite shows. He popped the first disc into the player and turned the TV on.

Falan had curled up in the corner of the sofa and looked at him in surprise when the disc loaded.

"You like this show?" she asked.

"Until work got in the way last year, I never missed an episode."

"Thankfully it comes on after I get home from work so I never miss it."

"You know, we've never asked you where you work."

"I'm the administrative assistant for Preston Somner and Forest Winters."

Nolen growled. "Fairies! You work for fairies?"

"Well, at the time they hired me, I didn't realize they were anything other than human. It was when I caught them using magic to write a contract that they told me the truth. What does it matter? They're incredibly kind. I couldn't have asked for better bosses."

"Have either of them ever made a pass at you?"

She snorted. "Have you seen the stick thin women they date? My thigh is bigger around than their waists. So no, they haven't ever made a pass at me."

Somewhat mollified, Nolen pulled her into his arms. "Sorry, sweetheart. The thought of you and other men makes me a little crazy."

"I already told you I've never had a boyfriend. If someone like Preston or Forest had been interested in me, don't you think they would've asked me out, and not taken no for an answer?"

He sighed. "I know. It's just going to take me a little time to adjust."

"Adjust?"

"To having a mate. A woman has never made me feel so crazy before."

She snuggled into him. "Take all the time you need. I'm not exactly used to having a man in my life, either, much less two. But I'm adjusting as quickly as I can."

They watched the rest of the show in silence until their food arrived. Nolen insisted on answering the door and paying. Judging by the delivery guy's shocked face, he had a feeling the news was going to spread -- one of the infamous Fitzgerald brothers was at Falan's house. It wasn't quite the way he wanted to break the news that he'd found his mate, but what was done was done.

* * *

They'd eaten and watched two episode of *Supernatural* and still hadn't heard from Brandt. Falan knew he was in a meeting, but just how long could a dinner meeting last? It made her wonder who he was having dinner with, but she wasn't about to ask Nolen. The last thing she wanted was to sound like a jealous girlfriend, or make him think she preferred

Brandt's company. She really was having a nice time with Nolen.

A glance at the clock showed it was after nine. Considering the day she'd had, she was more than ready to go to bed. Nolen still looked wide awake, but what she really wanted was for him to lie beside her and hold her. She needed to feel his arms around her.

"I think I'm going to turn in for the night," she said softly. "Are you staying?"

He ran his knuckles down her cheek. "I'd love to stay. But if we're going to bed, I need to text Brandt so he won't drive over thinking we're awake."

She nodded. "You do that while I change for bed."

She left him in the living room and went into the bathroom to wash her face and brush her teeth. When she was finished, she stepped into the bedroom and slipped on her purple silk nightie. She pulled down the covers and climbed into bed. A few minutes later, Nolen entered the room.

"Everything okay?" she asked.

"Fine. Brandt finally responded. The meeting is running over a bit so he said he'd see us in the morning."

She frowned. "Does this sort of thing happen often?"

"Sometimes dinner isn't long enough to discuss a renovation project and we end up taking them out for drinks afterward."

"So he's out drinking tonight?"

Nolen closed the bedroom door and pulled his shirt over his head. "It's just a meeting, sweetheart."

She shrugged and looked away. But when she heard his shoes hit the floor and then the rasp of a zipper, she found herself looking his way once more. She watched as he stripped out of the rest of his clothes and licked her lips. He really was a breathtaking man. And he was all hers!

Brandt and his meeting were completely forgotten as Nolen strode toward her. He leaned over her and she placed her hands on his bare chest. She felt the *thud* of his heart against her palms, but more than that, she felt his strength. She needed that strength right now. She needed *him*.

Nolen cupped her cheek and lowered his mouth to hers. He kissed her slowly, tenderly. Falan felt herself warming from the inside out. Nolen's kisses made her melt.

He slowly lifted her nightgown, dragging the silky material up her body. Lifting his mouth from hers, he removed the nightgown, tossing it on the floor. Her nipples tightened under his intense gaze. She watched as he pulled her panties down her legs. Laid bare, she trembled in anticipation. He knelt before her and pushed her legs apart. Falan nearly forgot to breathe at the first swipe of his tongue against her pussy. She felt him dip his tongue inside of her then drag it up to her clit. He circled the nub before sucking on it long and hard. Every nerve in her body was humming. As Nolen fucked her with his mouth, she felt herself getting closer and closer. Just when she thought she couldn't take any more, she came, flooding him with her juices.

She felt boneless she was so well-satisfied. But she knew there was more to come. Nolen quickly put on a condom and settled over her. She wrapped her legs around him. He entered her, stretching her, filling her. Her gaze held his as he pumped in and out of her. She placed her hands on his shoulders, feeling the muscles bunch and move with every thrust. The strength and masculine beauty of him took her breath away. As she gazed into his eyes, she felt her heart flutter and she wondered if she could be falling in love with him. He and Brandt had become her knights in shining armor. And she knew being their mate was sacred, a bond unlike any other on earth.

Nolen's strokes became harder, longer, deeper… And then she was flying. Her heart was racing and she was still free falling when he came calling her name. Holding him tight, she kissed him hungrily.

He pulled away and stood. Lifting her into his arms, he carried her into the bathroom. She flipped on the light switch when she passed it, and he set her on her feet. She watched as he turned on the shower and tested the water temperature. Then, he turned to her with those mesmerizing blue eyes and charming smile.

He held his hand out to her. "Let's get that delectable body of yours rinsed off."

She felt her cheeks heat in a blush and placed her hand in his. Stepping into the shower, she tugged his hand to pull him in behind her. She wasn't sure which felt better, the water rushing over her, or his hands sliding along her skin so smoothly, caressing every inch of her. When he reached for her shower gel, her skin warmed in anticipation. He lathered her from head to toe and then helped her rinse, his hands loving every inch of her.

Falan looked at the shower gel then up at Nolen. "Hope you don't mind smelling like jasmine."

He smiled. "I never mind smelling like you."

She washed him slowly, savoring the feel of his muscles under her palms. When she grasped his cock, she stroked it firmly, bringing it back to life. In the books she'd read, the men were always ready for round two almost immediately, but she didn't think that happened in real life. Nolen was proving that he could indeed go another round. The hardened length of him filled her hand and she suddenly wanted to know what he tasted like. Rinsing the soap from his body, she fell to her knees before him. With her gaze fastened on his, she leaned forward and licked the length of him. He hissed in a breath and fisted her hair, holding her back.

"Falan, sweetheart, what are you doing?"

"I wanted to see what you taste like. I want... I want to suck your cock."

He groaned and loosened his grip.

Falan cupped his balls and slowly took his cock in her mouth, sucking him to the back of her throat. She pulled back, her tongue curling around him. She'd only ever dreamed of doing something like this and she hoped she wasn't screwing it up. Her eyes met his again and the desire she saw there had her sucking longer and harder with each stroke. Her hand gripped his ass as she pulled him closer, taking him further down her throat. With her mouth full of cock, she swallowed.

"You're going to make me come, sweetheart."

Wanting that to happen very much, she doubled her efforts. Every time he bumped the back of her throat, she swallowed. Nolen fisted his hands in her hair, but he didn't try to direct her. She could tell by his breathing that he was close. She brought him to the brink and then he was coming, bathing her throat with his seed. She swallowed every drop, loving the flavor of him on her tongue.

"Falan, that was… incredible."

She licked her lips and rose to her feet. "It isn't like you've never had that done before."

"Not like that. Being with you is better than anything I've experienced before." He pulled her closer. "When we made love earlier, it felt like we were two souls becoming one. I've never felt so connected to anyone in my life before."

She rested her cheek on his chest. "I worried that I was the only one who felt that way."

"Come on, let's get dried off and into bed."

Nolen helped her from the shower and wrapped her in a fluffy towel. She wrung the water from her hair as she watched him dry off. After he tossed his towel in the hamper, he helped Falan finish drying her hair and body. He carried her into the bedroom and laid her down. Turning off all the lights, he slipped between the sheets and gathered her in his arms. She curled against his side, her head on his shoulder.

"Thank you for staying with me, Nolen."

"There's no place I'd rather be than by your side, Falan. If it were up to me, you'd move into our house tomorrow."

"But I'd be giving up my home."

He sighed. "I know, sweetheart. We'll figure it out. Get some sleep."

Nolen's arms tightened around her and before long she was drifting peacefully to sleep.

Chapter Five

The next morning a loud banging woke them, which Nolen quickly figured out was someone pounding on the front door. He eased himself out from under Falan, who was already drifting back to sleep, and pulled on his boxers before going to answer it. He peered through the peephole and saw his brother towering on the porch. Unlocking the door, he opened it and motioned Brandt inside.

"Here a little early, aren't you?" he asked.

Brandt scanned him from head to toe. "Did I interrupt something?"

"Yeah, sleep. Thankfully you didn't wake Falan, not really."

Brandt sniffed the air then looked at his brother with a grin. "I might not have interrupted something this morning, but you certainly enjoyed yourself last night, didn't you?"

"She needed to be loved."

"Is that what it was? Have you fallen in love with our mate?"

Nolen shrugged. "I think I might have fallen for her our first time together. But spending time with her last night, just the two of us… We didn't do anything spectacular before heading to bed, but I feel like we're closer now than we were before."

"Does that mean you've convinced her to move in with us?"

He shook his head. "She still wants her own home. But on the plus side, I think she wants us with her. She just isn't ready to let go of the familiar yet."

"So what, we take turns staying here at night?"

"We'll figure out something, Brandt. Right now, why don't you strip down and crawl into bed with her?"

"Maybe we should both go crawl into bed with her."

They moved toward the bedroom, Brandt removing clothes as they went. When they opened the door, Falan was in the middle of the bed, dead to the world. Nolen smiled at his twin before reclaiming the right side of the bed, pulling Falan up close. He felt the bed dip when Brandt crawled in on her other side, spooning her from behind. Knowing that his brother would want to play with their mate, Nolen kissed her awake.

"Morning," she murmured, peering up at him sleepily. Then she looked over her shoulder and smiled at Brandt.

"Since I didn't get to stop by last night, I figured I'd best get here first thing this morning," Brandt told her.

"I like waking up between you two."

Brandt kissed her shoulder. "What if we said we wanted to love you at the same time?"

"Then I'd say I want that, too."

Nolen looked at his brother over Falan's shoulder. "Did you bring anything with you?"

"It's out in the truck."

Nolen snorted. "Then I suggest you put some pants back on and take a trip outside."

Brandt rolled out of bed and pulled on his jeans. While he went to get some lube from the truck, Nolen snuggled Falan closer. He tucked her hair behind her ear and smoothed his thumb along her jaw. Leaning forward, he claimed her lips in a kiss.

Kissing his mate had become one of his favorite things to do.

"Are you sure this is what you want to do?" he asked her. "You're still new to all of this. If you need more time, we won't rush you."

"I'm sure, Nolen. My first time with both of you was wonderful, but I want to be with both of you at the same time."

Brandt returned and set the lube down on the bedside table. Taking off his jeans, he slipped into bed again, pulling Falan back against him. Nolen caressed her, sliding his hand down to her pussy. Delving between her legs, he thrust his fingers inside of her.

"Mmm. Someone's really wet this morning."

She blushed. "Maybe because someone woke up with her two favorite men in bed with her."

"Is that all it takes?" Nolen asked.

She cupped his cheek. "All it takes is me thinking about you two. Being in the same room with you just makes me wetter."

Brandt growled and nipped her shoulder. "I can't begin to tell you how much I want you right now."

"Then take me," she said breathlessly.

Both brothers put on condoms, then Nolen rolled her so that she sprawled across him. He kissed her hungrily while Brandt prepared her. He knew his brother was using more than just a little lube when he felt some drip on him. And he knew the moment his brother started playing with their mate's rosette. He felt her stiffen for a moment and then relax. He continued to kiss her and stroke his hands down her arms and back, keeping her focused on something other than the fingers moving in and out of her ass. He knew it would be uncomfortable for her the first time, but he wanted this more than anything.

When Brandt lifted her hips and lowered her onto Nolen's cock, he knew it was time. A thrill shot through him at the thought of sharing this beautiful woman, *their* woman, with his brother. They'd shared women before, but it could never compare to this moment.

"Just relax, sweetheart," he said as he held her close. "Push out against him and let him in."

It took a minute or two, but finally, he felt his brother enter her completely. Falan gasped and arched her back.

"I feel so full. Do something, anything!"

With a grin, he withdrew. As he surged back in, he felt his brother pull out. Working in tandem, they brought her pleasure. The look of surprise and bliss on her face only fueled his desire. He reached up to tweak her nipples and felt her tremble.

A look at his brother over her shoulder told him that Brandt wouldn't last much longer. Being with their mate had been incredible each time, but this... this was heaven on earth. He'd never felt so connected to anyone in his life, and to share this experience with his brother and the woman he loved -- and yes, he could admit he loved her -- was beyond amazing.

He felt Falan tense and knew she was about to come. Reaching between their bodies, he teased her clit, circling the sensitive nub. Her trembling intensified and then she was coming, flooding him with her juices. The rush of liquid heat enveloping him pushed him over the edge and he tumbled into orgasm, his brother following. She came again, calling out their names.

Brandt withdrew first, gently tracing her back. He had a look of awe on his face and Nolen wondered what put it there, other than the amazing moment they'd just shared with Falan. He had a feeling there was more to it, but before he could ask, his brother was moving quickly to the bathroom. He returned a moment later with a warm wet rag and began cleaning their mate. Nolen watched as his brother kissed their mate and felt a sense of peace, of rightness. Knowing they would have many more mornings like this one made him happier than he'd been in a long time.

"I'll shower first," he offered, knowing his brother wanted some time with Falan.

Brandt nodded and gathered Falan in his arms.

Nolen smiled, rising from the bed. But as he turned to look at them one last time, he froze. On Falan's back was no longer just a crescent moon. She now bore the full mark of a mated woman, a woman carrying their child. He was more than a little dazed as he left them. How had it happened? Had the condom leaked? If so, he hadn't noticed. Despite the fact that they hadn't discussed children, everything was right in his world. Well, almost everything. They still had to find Falan's stalker. But with the pack working along with the police, surely the mystery would be solved soon enough. And now knowing she was carrying their child, he was more determined than ever to put a stop to the person trying to take her from them.

* * *

Brandt kissed Falan, holding her close. He was thankful that this amazing woman was in his life, and he was more than a little in love with her already. He just wasn't sure if it was the right moment to tell her. Would she think he was telling her only because of the incredible lovemaking they'd just shared? That was the last thing he wanted.

He was glad his brother had given him this time alone with her. While it was true he'd had some time with her that first night, it hadn't been enough. He knew Nolen had been intimate with her last night, but he didn't feel cheated. He knew there would be times in the future when it would be him lying with her, and other times they'd share her. Sometimes they'd take her together like they just had, and other times they would take turns like they had their first time together. But no matter the circumstances of their joining, it would be extraordinary every single time.

She snuggled close to him and he held her tight. It felt right, holding her in his arms. She was his perfect match, his mate, his life. While he was enjoying the afterglow, he knew it wouldn't last. Reality would intrude sooner or later. Already his mind was on the threat to her life, wondering what he could do to keep her safe.

"You're thinking awfully hard," she said.

"Just wondering what I ever did to deserve having someone so wonderful in my life."

"I'm not that wonderful. I have flaws."

"I haven't seen any."

She laughed. "You just haven't been around me enough."

He smoothed her hair back from her face. "We could change that. You could move in with us. I know you like your independence, and I know you want to keep your home, but there's going to come a time when you'll have to move in with us. We can't live separately forever. That isn't how this relationship is going to work."

"I know," she said softly. "I just don't think I'm ready for that step yet."

"There's something you should know."

"What?"

"Your mark… it's complete now."

She grew still in his arms. "Complete? I don't understand. What's that mean? I thought it was already complete."

"It means you're carrying our child now. It's more important than ever that we protect you. And we can't do that if we're not here with you."

Brandt watched as she digested that bit of information. Condoms weren't fool proof and it seemed she was coming to the same conclusion. But would she be happy about having a baby with them? It was rather sudden and they were still getting to know one another.

"But one of you will always be here; you agreed to take turns staying with me."

"Yes, but you'd be safer with both of us around."

"Please, Brandt. I don't want to discuss this now."

"All right, but it's a discussion that will happen sooner or later. Once Nolen sees your mark, he'll want to move you into our home, too."

She snuggled into his embrace and he held her tight. One way or another they had to convince her to move in with them. If something happened to her… he didn't even want to think about living without her.

Nolen returned from his shower and smiled at them. "Shower's free if someone else wants to get cleaned up."

Brandt released her and rolled out of bed, only to lift her into his arms a moment later. "No reason we can't shower together."

She held on tight as he carried her out of the room, but Nolen followed.

"Is there something you'd like to share with me?" he asked.

Brandt set her down and started the shower. "You mean about her mark? I figured you'd already seen it."

Nolen nodded. "I did. But how does everyone else feel about it?"

He glanced at Falan. "I'm okay with it, but I think she's still processing it."

Nolen pulled her into his arms. "How do you feel about it, sweetheart?"

"I'm happy, but I'm also a little scared. If that woman is after me because she thinks I've stolen you, what's she going to do when she finds out I'm pregnant?"

Brandt and Nolen shared a look. Honestly, he hadn't thought of that. He knew they had more to worry about now, but he hadn't thought about the woman learning of the pregnancy. If Falan kept her mark covered, there was no reason anyone had to know about it. Except, perhaps, Hayden. They did need to contact him and let him know that it was now more important than ever to protect Falan.

"Call Hayden while we're getting cleaned up," Brandt told Nolen. "He needs to know about the baby."

Nolen nodded and backed out of the bathroom.

Falan stepped into the shower and Brandt followed. He watched the water flow over her body and felt his cock begin to rise again. He wouldn't take her, not this soon, but he couldn't deny that he wanted her. Reaching for her shampoo, he helped her lather and rinse her hair before soaping her body. His hands glided over her smooth satiny skin. After helping her rinse, he quickly washed himself before turning off the water.

As they dried off, his gaze caressed her lush curves. He wondered, not for the first time, how he'd gotten so lucky. The fates had chosen well when they'd selected her for his mate. Not only was she beautiful, but she was kind. Never had he met a sweeter woman than his Falan. While it was true that he wanted her every time he was near her, he was also satisfied just holding her or being near her. He was content just looking at her, knowing that she was his.

Sure, he shared her with his brother, but he didn't feel the slightest bit jealous.

"Are you sore?" he asked.

"A little."

"It will get easier each time we're together. Your body will adjust to us."

She smiled at him. "I didn't say that I didn't enjoy myself, only that I was a little bit sore. I'm sure it will pass soon."

He pulled her into his arms and kissed her. "Have I told you how amazing you are?"

"Not in the last hour."

"Well, you are, and I'm lucky to have you in my life. I know we just met, but I've come to care about you a great deal, Falan."

"I care about you, too."

"I think we're going to do well together, the three of us. I know everything is new to you, but you're adjusting well, faster than I had hoped. And now that you're expecting…"

"Is this where you point out again that I should move in with you?"

He grinned. "I get the feeling it wouldn't do me any good, so no, I won't do that. But know that you're welcome in our home anytime you desire to make our relationship a bit more official. You're marked, but the pack is going to think it a bit odd that you haven't moved in with us. And since they can't see the mark, they're not going to understand why we're with you so much. They don't understand that you're our mate, even though we've told our alpha about you."

"So, what, they think I'm your girlfriend? Or just someone you're passing time with?"

"Since we've never spent this much time with one woman before, I'm not sure what they'll make of it. I guess it's possible they'll assume you're our mate even though they can't see your mark, but they'll wonder until you move in with us, or until they see our marks."

She frowned. "I don't like the idea of the women in the pack thinking you're single."

He smiled. "You have nothing to fear. Knowing that our mate wasn't part of our pack, we've avoided the female werewolves. We didn't want our mate to feel uncomfortable at pack gatherings once we found her, or them since we thought we were looking for two separate women. It never occurred to us that we would share a mate."

"Have you… have you shared women before? You seemed to know what you were doing."

He hesitated. Something told him she wasn't going to like the answer he was going to give, but he wasn't about to lie to her.

"Yes, we've shared women before. But nothing could ever compare to being with you, Falan. Being with you… it's the most incredible experience of my life, and I know that Nolen feels the same way."

"Really?"

He caressed her cheek. "Really."

She seemed satisfied with his answer and they entered the bedroom to get dressed. Nolen was nowhere in sight so Brandt assumed he was in the living room, probably watching TV if he knew his brother. They dressed quickly, but Falan took time to fix her hair and put on some make-up. Brandt assured her she didn't need any, but she refused to listen.

When they joined Nolen, he was sprawled in the corner of the sofa with his feet kicked up on the coffee table. Falan frowned at him and he immediately dropped his feet to the floor.

"I thought we'd all go out for breakfast."

Brandt looked at the clock on the wall. "It's nearly ten o'clock. Most places are going to start serving lunch soon."

"There's that new IHOP that just opened over on Elmwood. I think they serve breakfast all day."

Brandt nodded and looked at Falan. "Does that sound good to you?"

Her stomach chose that moment to rumble and both brothers grinned. She blushed prettily.

"I think Falan's stomach agrees," Nolen said. "Whose truck are we taking?"

"Mine's probably cleaner," Brandt said, thinking of the last time he'd ridden with his brother and the empty coffee cups that had littered the floor.

Nolen gave them a sheepish look. "You're right. Mine's a mess."

Brandt grabbed his keys off the counter that separated her kitchen from her living room and motioned for them to head out.

Chapter Six

Breakfast was pleasant. Falan had enjoyed learning more about the brothers and their childhood antics. She'd tried to find out more about their adult lives, but they'd clammed up and she'd wondered if it had anything to do with the women they'd seen throughout the years. She knew they'd been more into one night stands than relationships, but surely they hadn't been with *that* many women, had they? It made her feel a little insecure despite what Brandt had said to her earlier. She knew she needed to conquer her insecurities and that she needed to learn how to value herself more, but it was an uphill battle. She was already feeling better about her weight after having been around the brothers for a few days, but she also knew she'd never be skinny. Her mother had been a large woman and she knew it was just in her genes. It did make her wonder just how large she was going to get now that she was pregnant. She didn't think her stomach had much more room to grow.

Falan wondered what she could do to please them more in the bedroom. Not having been with men before she didn't have a clue as to what to do. Sure, she'd read romance novels, but they only helped so much. She'd always been too bashful to check out the erotic romance books, or the ménages, but maybe it was time to conquer that shyness and pick up a few. Maybe she'd learn something she could use to make her men happy. She could just imagine how surprised they'd be. But with them shadowing her every move, she knew it would be a while before she would get to a bookstore, especially alone, and she definitely wanted her newfound knowledge to be a surprise.

She'd told them about her childhood, the teasing she'd endured, the lack of dates. She'd even confessed that it had been hard for her to make friends until she'd reached high school. But even the friends she'd made then hadn't stuck around, most had moved away and she'd lost contact with them. She'd felt so blessed when she'd met Stella and then she too had moved away. Falan hadn't really had many friends since then. She'd been lonely, but she knew she had people who cared about her. The Leicesters for one. It had been kind of them to rent her the small cottage for such a reasonable price, and she loved her home. But other than exchanging pleasantries when she saw them, and receiving a Christmas ham every year, she had little contact with her landlords. Their daughter was friendly enough, but Falan had been too shy to try and make friends.

As they pulled down the winding driveway to her home, she noticed smoke. It seemed a little warm to have a fire burning, and it also seemed a little too far off from the main house. Worry knotted her stomach. She had a very bad feeling.

As they got closer to her home, she knew her fears were well founded. The outside of her home was scorched and the inside looked charred. The living room was caving in and fire licked the walls and windows. The Leicesters were out front, their son on his cell phone, she assumed to call the fire department. But she knew it was too late. Everything she'd ever owned was in that house and now it was nothing but ash.

The moment the truck stopped she bolted out the door and ran to her home. Strong arms wrapped around her from behind, pulling her back against a hard chest. She knew by instinct that Nolen had her.

Tears silently trickled down her cheeks. She saw people talking, but she couldn't hear anything, nothing but the crackling of the fire.

All at once, everything snapped into focus and the sound came rushing back. She heard Brandt talking to the Leicesters about the fire, heard their son speaking to the fire department dispatcher, and Nolen was murmuring in her ear.

"Easy, Falan. You can't go rushing in there, sweetheart. You'll get hurt."

"How could she do this, Nolen? How could she burn my home?"

"I don't know, but we're going to find out who did this and we're going to make her pay. I promise you she won't go unpunished."

First the warning, then her tires, now her home. What was left? What else could the woman possibly take from her? She had nothing left. She turned in Nolen's embrace and sobbed against his shirt, holding him tight. What if she'd been in the house when the fire had started? What if… She froze.

"Nolen, your truck was out front. Do you think she thought we were inside?"

She felt his heart skip a beat.

"Jesus, Falan. I want to think that isn't possible, but… we definitely need to call the police and Hayden. I don't think this was just arson. I think you're right, this was attempted murder."

She clung to him, truly frightened. It seemed the game had taken a deadly turn. What would happen when the woman realized she'd failed? Would she try again? And how could she possibly try to kill Nolen if he was the one she was after? Did that mean it was Brandt she'd wanted all along? Or had she finally slipped over the edge and lost all reasoning? Maybe she no longer cared if she had Nolen, maybe she'd decided if she couldn't have him no one could. The thought chilled Falan.

Brandt, having heard them, pulled out his cell phone and called both the police and their alpha. This time he requested their best trackers. Hopefully there was a trail that could be followed, but if the perpetrator was part of their pack, then she would know they would attempt to follow her and she would cover her tracks. But they had to try. Anything to keep Falan safe. The brothers were truly afraid for their mate. Nolen knew he couldn't lose her, not after having just found her.

"You're coming with us now for sure," he told her. "We won't take no for an answer."

She nodded. "I have nothing... no clothes, no shoes, no make-up..."

"You don't need the make-up," Nolen told her. "But we can replace the rest. I'm sure you had small things, momentos from your mother that can't be replaced, but everything else we'll take care of."

"I can't let you do that. I had my purse with me so I have my checkbook. I can buy my own things."

"Please, let us do this for you, Falan. We almost lost you. If you'd been in there..."

She understood. Just the thought of Nolen trapped in that house was more than she could bear. If they needed to pamper her to feel better, she'd let them. And she agreed, the best place for her was in their home. With them by her side, surely she would be safe.

She glanced at the charred house once more. Then again, maybe not. If the woman was willing to kill Nolen, there was no reason she wouldn't kill Brandt, too. No one was safe while that woman was on the loose. Until they found her, they would have to be on their guard. She wasn't sure she'd ever sleep again, not until she knew they were safe.

Nolen led her away from the house. He lowered the tailgate on Brandt's truck and lifted her onto it. He took her hands in his and kissed them. She knew he was trying to comfort her, but she wasn't sure anything could make her feel better just then, not while she was so worried.

Sirens sounded and she watched as the fire trucks came into view. There wasn't much they could do at this point except put out the last of the dying flames. The house couldn't be salvaged. If the Leicesters decided they wanted to keep a cottage on their property, they would have to tear down what was left of the structure and rebuild. She felt like it was her fault. She knew she had no control over what was going on, but she knew that if she'd never met Nolen and Brandt, had never brought them home, then none of this would be happening.

She paused. Was that the answer? Would they all be safe if she took a step back? She didn't want to let them go, but perhaps that would be best for everyone involved. It would mean the woman would win, and she hated that more than anything, but she couldn't sit back and let her try again. What if she succeeded next time? What if she killed Brandt and Nolen?

Tears gathered in her eyes and she looked at Nolen. He smoothed her hair back from her face and caressed her cheek. It would break her heart to let him go, to let both of them go, but what other choice did she have? She couldn't see another way out of this mess.

"I think it would be best if I went to a hotel," she said softly.

He frowned. "A hotel? We have plenty of room, Falan. You'll be safer with us."

She fought to keep her tears at bay, but knew they were close to spilling over. "I think... I think maybe we need to take a break."

"A break? What exactly does that mean?"

"It means we shouldn't see each other anymore."

He growled. "You're carrying our child. *My* child. Do you honestly think I'm just going to let you walk away? Is that what you really want?"

"It's the only way! Don't you see? She isn't going to stop, Nolen. The only way to keep you safe, both of you, is if I go away. If we stop seeing each other, then she'll leave you alone."

"No, that isn't an option."

Brandt walked up. "What isn't an option?"

"She wants to leave."

"So take her home. I'm sure I can handle the police when they arrive."

"No, she wants to leave *us*. She thinks if she isn't around anymore that we'll be safe. She wants to walk away."

Brandt narrowed his eyes and growled at her. "No."

"But it's the only way," she said. "You have to see that."

"We're not giving you up, Falan. There's only one mate in the world for each of us, and you happen to be ours. We're not losing you and our child. You mean too much to us," Brandt said.

Her tears trickled down her cheeks and she fought back a sob. "I don't want to go, but I need to."

Nolen pulled her into his arms. "The only place you need to go is home with me. But first, we need to replace some of your things. We can do a more thorough shopping trip another day, but you need the bare necessities."

She sniffled and nodded. She still felt that everyone would be safer if she weren't around, but she knew she couldn't argue with them. Especially since she didn't really want to leave them. She wanted to spend the rest of her life with them, and she hated that some psychotic woman was making her feel like she couldn't.

Nolen helped her down and led her over to his truck. "I have to warn you, it's messy."

She grinned. "I could just follow you in my car."

"We'll have one of the pack members drive it over, just leave your keys with Brandt."

She pulled them out and handed them over. Brandt leaned down and kissed her cheek before helping her into the truck. She shoved empty coffee cups and a Danish wrapper or two out of the way. They hadn't lied when they said Nolen's truck was a mess. It made her want to grab a plastic bag and start throwing things away.

Buckled and ready to go, she waved to Brandt as Nolen turned around and drove away. She looked in the side view mirror at her house one last time. She would miss her home, but she knew this day was coming. She'd known there was no way for her to be their mate, to carry their child, and not live with them.

Whether she was ready or not, it was time to face the next phase of her life.

* * *

After picking up a few changes of clothes and another pair of shoes, Nolen had driven them home. She looked up at the two-story gray house and thought that it looked rather plain and lonely. If she was going to live here, she was going to have her work cut out for her. The first thing she wanted to do was paint the house, then work on planting some flowers and shrubs. There wasn't even a tree in sight. How had they lived like this?

Nolen looked at her and then the house. "I know it isn't much, but it has some potential, I think. Can you be happy here?"

"Well, it certainly needs some work. Expect a rather lengthy 'honey do' list, but yes, I can be happy here."

He grinned. "You make as many lists as you want. We'll do whatever you want as long as you're happy."

Falan got out of the truck and followed Nolen up the walkway to the front door. It was just a plain white door with a peephole, but she could easily envision a prettier door with beveled or etched glass. When they entered the house, she looked around, taking everything in. They stood in an entry hall with stairs in front of them, a living room to their left and a dining room to their right. The kitchen was straight back. She assumed all of the bedrooms were upstairs.

"Feel free to wander around a bit while I bring your things in," Nolen told her. "There are four bedrooms upstairs, but we're putting your things in the master bedroom."

"Where do you and Brandt sleep?"

"We have our own rooms."

"Oh." She wasn't sure what else to say. Did they plan on keeping separate rooms, or were they going to share the master bedroom with her?

He grinned. "I can see the wheels turning in your mind. We'll discuss sleeping arrangements later."

She meandered through the first floor while Nolen brought in her shopping bags, then she followed him upstairs. There was wall to wall beige carpet on both floors and the walls were nearly the same color. She'd never been in such a depressing house before. How did they stand it?

The master bedroom was at the end of the hall. Even with the king size bed, dresser and bedside tables, the room was spacious. There was a door to the right and she went to open it. The bathroom was just as beige and blah as the rest of the house, but it did boast a large garden tub, easily big enough for three, and a large shower. On the opposite end of the bathroom were two doors. She peeked inside and saw two gigantic closets. Perhaps the house had some redeeming qualities after all, other than the two hunky werewolves who lived in it.

"What do you think?" Nolen asked.

"My honest opinion?"

He winced. "That doesn't sound good."

"It's awfully beige. Be prepared to do lots of painting. But the room sizes are nice. I love the closets and the bathtub, and I don't hate the furniture." She smiled. "It's definitely something I can work with."

He breathed a sigh of relief. "Good. I was worried we would have to move."

She laughed. "No, I wouldn't make you give up your home. I just need a little color around me. And maybe a few touches like pictures, some flowers or plants, and a couple of decorative candles or something. Just some things to make it a bit more homey."

Nolen pulled her into his arms. "Sweetheart, you nest to your heart's content. We'll buy you whatever you want and paint whatever you want."

"You may change your mind after you've painted nearly every room in the house, and replaced the carpet."

"The carpet?"

"I've always wanted hardwood floors."

He groaned. "You do like to torture us, don't you?"

"It can't be that bad. People lay hardwood floors all the time."

"Most of the time it's laminate or those floors that snap together. If we put in hardwood floors, you better believe we're doing it the right way. In case you forgot, we're in the renovation business. We can't expect people to pay for the best in their homes if we don't have the best in ours."

She gave the walls and carpet a pointed look.

"Okay, so we haven't done anything with the place. Maybe we were just waiting for you."

She kissed him. "Good answer."

A door closed downstairs and she started to pull away.

"It's just Brandt," Nolen said. "He'll be up in a minute."

Sure enough, she heard footsteps on the stairs and a moment later Brandt appeared in the doorway. He looked tense and she wondered how the meeting had gone with the police and Hayden.

"How did shopping go?" he asked.

"Fine. How did everything go with the police?" Nolen asked.

"They don't have any leads, but I didn't expect they would. Hayden came by with two trackers. They scouted the area, but the trail went cold about a mile from the cottage. The good news is that the trackers have her scent now. Unfortunately, there's about eighty people in the pack and they can hardly go around sniffing every female they see."

"What about the guy Hayden left guarding the place?" Nolen asked.

"Someone stopped to ask him for directions so he didn't see anything. By the time the person had moved along, the fire had already started."

"Why didn't he call the fire department?"

"He was too busy trying to find the person responsible for the fire. He thought that would be a better use of his time, but she had too much of a head start. By the time he found the place where she'd stashed her car, she was long gone. Hayden really let him have it, pointing out it would have only taken a moment to call the fire department and he could've done that while he was hunting the perpetrator."

Falan sighed. "Are we ever going to find her?"

"She'll slip up. We just have to be patient," Nolen said.

Falan shook her head. "I don't think we have that luxury. If we'd been in that house today, we'd be dead."

Nolen kissed her. "We'll ask for guards. More than one should keep her from getting to you again."

Falan leaned into him. She had to put her trust in them. She may have lost her home, but she was still alive and she knew that Brandt and Nolen would do everything in their power to keep her safe. But it didn't stop her from worrying. She knew she would worry until the woman was caught.

"Come on," Nolen said. "Let's walk through the house and you can tell us what you want each room to look like. It will give us an idea of what kind of work we have ahead of us, and it will keep your troubles off your mind."

She kissed him again. "You're going to regret asking me to do that."

He grinned. "Maybe. We can start with the bedrooms."

She paused. "Speaking of the bedrooms… I don't like the idea of you two sleeping apart from me. Would you want to move in here with me?"

"I can't think of anything we'd like more, baby," Brandt told her. "We'll work on moving our things this afternoon."

Chapter Seven

True to their word, the brothers had moved their belongings into the master bedroom, sharing the second closet. After Falan had run through a list of what she'd like to do with the house, they'd taken her out to lunch and then spent the rest of the afternoon relaxing at home. Brandt had called Hayden and arranged to have two guards posted outside of the house at all times, but Falan wondered what would happen when she went to work the next day. Surely they didn't expect someone to shadow her everywhere she went.

They hadn't really discussed what would happen when Monday came. Both brothers would go back to work and so would she, but Falan didn't think they'd really thought about that. Whether they liked it or not, she was returning to her job. She might not have rent to pay any longer, but she still had other bills. Credit cards, a car payment, insurance… she couldn't just sit home and twiddle her thumbs.

Besides, she enjoyed her job. Her bosses were agreeable men, both had been super nice to her since the day they'd hired her. She couldn't imagine working anywhere else. She splayed a hand across her stomach. Now that she was pregnant she wasn't sure what would happen with her job. They'd never discussed maternity leave when she'd been hired because she hadn't been seeing anyone, much less had prospects for a permanent relationship and children. Hopefully her bosses would hold her job for her while she was out. But she had plenty of time to think about that. She had to be honest with them, of course, and let them know she was expecting, but she didn't have to make long term plans yet.

It was still hard to believe there was a baby in there. She wondered if she was going to experience morning sickness, cravings, would she grow big as a house… all of the things she'd heard about on TV or read about in the many romance novels she'd read. She was excited about the baby and looked forward to her pregnancy. The thought of making Nolen and Brandt go for midnight ice cream runs and setting up the nursery made her smile.

Her cell phone rang from inside her purse, drawing her out of her musings. She rummaged through the large bag and pulled it out. She recognized the number and ringtone immediately, smiling when she realized it was one of her huggable bosses, and answered quickly. She'd loved working for Forest and Preston, couldn't imagine any job she'd rather have. They'd always been supportive and had become more friends than employers.

"Hello."

"Falan, it's Forest Winters. I heard about the fire at your place and wanted to make sure you were okay."

"I'm fine, Forest. Thank you for calling to check on me."

"Why don't you take a few days off to get things sorted?"

"That's really kind of you, but I think it would be better if I worked."

There was silence for a moment. "I've also heard that you've been hanging around the Fitzgerald brothers."

News certainly travelled fast. "Yes, I have been."

"I know you're rather innocent, Falan, so I'm going to give you some advice. Find someone a little tamer, someone who can commit to you."

"Oh, I don't think you understand, Forest. They are committed to me."

"They?"

She blushed at his tone. "Yes. You see, I'm their mate."

"To both of them? That's rather unusual."

"Yes, well… despite that, things are working out well. I'm happy with the arrangement, happy with them. I know about their past and I'm sure that I'm not the type of woman they'd typically date, but I've come to care for them a great deal and I believe they feel the same."

"Good. I'm glad that things have worked out so well for you, burned house aside."

"About that… it seems that someone, a woman who wants Nolen, is after me. She's the one who set the fire. She also left a warning on my house the first night I met them and slashed my tires. The tire issue has been resolved, thanks to Brandt and Nolen, but the house is gone."

"Falan, I don't like the sound of that. You definitely need to stay home for a day or two. Take some time to enjoy your new relationship, get settled a bit in your new life, and focus on being happy. But most importantly, stay safe! You know Preston and I will protect you when you return to work, but I really think you need this time at home right now."

She sighed. "All right. I'll stay home, but just for a few days. I'll go stir crazy if I have to stay home all week."

He chuckled. "Very well. I'll see you Thursday."

"Goodbye, Forest."

"Bye, Falan."

She disconnected the call and stared at her phone a moment. Now what was she going to do? She wasn't used to having so much time to herself. She knew that Brandt and Nolen would be working, which meant she'd be alone in the house for those three days. Glancing around the room, she decided she could give the place a good scrubbing, but even that wouldn't take more than a day.

With a smile, she realized it was the perfect opportunity for her research. She'd go to the bookstore first thing Monday and spend Tuesday and Wednesday reading. Maybe she'd learn something new she could use with the guys before the weekend arrived, assuming she could convince them to make love to her before Friday night came. They didn't seem like the type to keep to a schedule, but she couldn't be sure.

Having her days planned, she curled up on the sofa and flipped through the TV channels while she waited on Brandt and Nolen to come back inside. They'd stepped out a half hour ago saying they had to work on something in the garage and she hadn't seen them since. She'd thought about peeking, but decided to leave them be. If they wanted her to know what they were up to, they'd tell her.

* * *

Night had fallen quickly and Falan had found herself exhausted. She'd crawled into bed long before Brandt and Nolen, hugging her pillow as she waited on her two wolves to join her, but she'd fallen asleep before they'd slipped into bed.

Waking slowly, she blinked against the bright light filtering in from the large bedroom window. She reached a hand out beside her and found that the bed was empty. She wondered how long she'd been alone in the large bed. She felt bereft, knowing she'd missed seeing them after they'd come to bed last night and missed seeing them off to work this morning. Why hadn't they woken her?

She pushed the covers aside and rose. She had a busy day planned and couldn't wait to begin. Throwing on a ragged pair of shorts and a tank top she'd confiscated from one of the guys' drawers, she went downstairs to hunt for cleaning supplies. Seeing as how the house wasn't completely trashed, she figured they had to have some somewhere. It was in the laundry room that she found what she was looking for, cleansers and furniture polish. Most of it looked new and she wondered just how often the guys had bothered cleaning, much less polishing anything.

Grabbing the necessary items, she started on the kitchen, scrubbing the counters, cabinets and appliances. After giving the floor a good mopping, she moved on to the living room. It took her several hours to clean the entire downstairs, complete with vacuuming, but she was proud of the work she'd done and smiled as she appraised her accomplishment. Everything gleamed and smelled citrusy.

In dire need of a shower, she hurried upstairs. She scrubbed herself and washed her hair before turning off the water. After she dried off, she towel dried her hair and brushed it well. She dug through the cabinets but couldn't find a hair dryer anywhere so she braided the thick mass.

No longer having the luxury of make-up, she dressed quickly in jeans and a red short-sleeve top before slipping on a pair of high-heeled black sandals. Anxious to begin her errands, she hurried downstairs and grabbed her purse and keys. She snatched the spare house keys from the hook beside the door and stepped out onto the porch, locking the door behind her.

She cautiously looked around before getting into her car, still not feeling safe after the fire and other incidents. It didn't take her long to drive from the Fitzgerald's house, which she supposed was now her house as well, to the hardware store. She immediately went to the paint section and contemplated what she wanted to do to each room of her new home.

It took her a good half hour to make her selections, but she walked out with several samples. Her next stop was the bookstore, Moonspell Books & More. She found she was looking forward to finding some ménage books, and even more so to reading them. But it seemed her quest was harder to accomplish than she'd thought. There was a small selection of erotic romance novels, but none of them were ménages. She stopped a sales clerk.

"Excuse me, I can't seem to find the books I'm looking for."

The woman smiled. "What can I help you find?"

Falan blushed. "I was hoping you might have some ménage romance books."

"Ah! We actually don't carry those in the store. Your best bet would be downloading them online and reading them on an e-reader."

"I don't have one of those."

"That's easy enough to fix." The woman motioned for her to follow as she walked toward the other end of the store. "We carry several different models. Do you know where you'll do most of your shopping?"

"Well, whenever I can't get a book here, I order it on Amazon."

"Then you'll probably want a Kindle. They're easy to use and affordable. The basic one is under one hundred dollars if you don't mind not having a touch screen."

Falan looked at the different e-readers, feeling slightly overwhelmed. Electronics tended to do that to her. She always despaired when it came time to purchase a new computer, which she'd now have to do thanks to the fire. And she didn't even want to think about what she'd gone through when she'd selected her cell phone. She just wasn't the type who liked gadgets.

Picking up the basic Kindle, she studied the box. It seemed straight forward enough, surely she could figure it out. She looked back up at the wall and noticed there were various covers and sleeves for all of the e-readers. After a little contemplation, she selected a pretty red cover for her new Kindle. If she was going to go to the trouble of buying it, she might as well make sure she protected it.

She thanked the woman and headed to the front with her items. It definitely wasn't what she'd hoped to buy, but maybe this would open up a whole new world of books for her. Now she could just download the books she wanted instead of having them shipped from Amazon. Something told her she was about to start reading a whole lot more.

Her purchase secured in a plastic sack, she stowed the bag in the front seat of her car. A glance at the clock in the dashboard showed that it was nearly four o'clock. She had no idea what time the guys would get home from work and she didn't want to be gone when they arrived. She had a feeling they would worry if she wasn't there.

It only took her fifteen minutes to arrive home. She'd noticed someone following her throughout the day and figured it was the guard the guys had mentioned, but she'd somehow lost them on the way home. She parked the car and gathered her things. Getting the house keys out of her purse, she unlocked the door and set her bags inside the door. While she was out, she figured she might as well get the mail. But as she turned, someone place a cloth over her nose and mouth. She struggled, but strong arms held her prisoner. The chemicals on the cloth began to work and her eyes slid shut as she sank into unconsciousness.

* * *

Brandt and Nolen frowned at the open door at home. Brandt looked back at the driveway and noted that Falan's car was, indeed, parked out front. A feeling of dread settled over him. She'd gone shopping and her bags were inside the door. Surely she wouldn't have left the door standing wide open.

"Falan?" Nolen called out as he stepped inside of the house.

Brandt sniffed the air. His eyes narrowed and he growled. "Do you smell that?"

Nolen sniffed. "Chloroform? Why would…"

Brandt slammed his fist into the wood frame of the door. "Someone has her."

"I'm calling Hayden now. We need trackers. All of them."

Brandt nodded and walked around the house, hoping to sniff out the path they'd taken. If they were lucky, they'd find her soon. If not… he didn't even want to think about what would happen if they couldn't find her. Someone wanted her dead, and this time they might actually succeed. Ice crept through his veins at the thought of never seeing her again.

Nolen disconnected and Brandt looked at him expectantly.

"We'll have four trackers here in the next fifteen minutes, and Hayden is coming as well. One way or another we'll find her, we just have to believe that."

Brandt gave a quick nod, not wanting to voice his doubts. They hadn't been able to track the woman up to this point so why would this day be any different? His heart ached at the loss of his mate. They shouldn't have left her alone. What had they been thinking? They hadn't been, obviously.

He sat on the top step and stretched out his long legs. It was obvious Falan had been taken, but where and to what purpose? If they were going to kill her, why not just do it at the house where they could find her body? Was there something else they had planned for her? The thought of the possible horrors she was facing was enough to make him sick.

A large SUV pulled up in the driveway and four guys stepped out. Brandt wasn't familiar with two of them, but he recognized David and Evan. He pushed himself off the steps and stood to greet them. He felt Nolen's presence behind him and knew his brother was just as anxious for the trackers to get started so they could find their mate.

Evan approached first and held out his hand, shaking first Brandt's and then Nolen's. "Good to see you guys, even if it is under bad circumstances. Have you met Seaton and Xander before?"

Brandt shook his head and offered his hand to the two new wolves. "It's a pleasure to meet you both."

"It's best if we get started before the trail gets too cold," Seaton said. "Where do you think she was abducted?"

"The front door was open and her things were just inside. There was a smell of chloroform on the porch. I followed it down the steps, but after that it died," Brand said. "Do you think you can follow it?"

The trackers looked at each other. David made his way onto the porch and stepped inside the house. "I'm going to shift and lead the others. Since we don't know what we're walking into, it's best if everyone else stays in human form."

Brandt shoved his hands in his pockets, feeling rather helpless at the moment, a feeling he didn't like. It should be him changing and tracking Falan, but he knew the trackers were better equipped to handle the job. They had the best noses in the pack and would be able to sniff her out faster. If anyone could find her, they could.

David materialized a moment later, a large red wolf. The other three trackers fell into step behind him. The wolf sniffed the air and then the ground. He glanced over his shoulder at the men before moving across the lawn. Brandt looked at Nolen. He had a feeling the trackers wanted them to stay put, but he wasn't about to let them find Falan while he was sitting on his ass.

They followed behind, keeping their distance but staying close enough to be of some use to Falan when they found her. And Brandt was determined it would be *when* and not *if*. One way or another, he would hold Falan in his arms again, and he would make sure that whoever had taken her would pay, and pay dearly.

It took nearly an hour, but finally they stopped in front of an old rundown clapboard home in a not so great part of town. There were lights on in the front rooms and the back of the house was black as pitch. The trackers sniffed the air around the home then huddled up near an oak in the front yard.

"There's definitely more than one person in there," Evan said.

Xander narrowed his eyes. "Yeah, and I recognize the scent of one of them. Fulton Sedgewick."

Seaton growled. "And Rebecca Laymont."

Brandt was more than a little surprised. Rebecca had followed him and his brother around quite a bit, but he would never have guessed her to be capable of something like this. She'd always seemed sweet and quiet. That she was the instigator in all of the crimes against his mate infuriated him.

"There's a third one," David said. "The scent is familiar, but not enough for me to put a face or name to it. I can just tell there's a second male inside."

Seaton looked at Brandt and Nolen. "We're going to go in and subdue them. Don't come in until you see one of us motion to you. Falan's scent is faint, but I can tell she's in there. We'll let you go to her just as soon as the criminals are taken care of."

Xander grinned. "You might want to go ahead and call Hayden, since he never showed at the house. He'll need to come clean up the mess when we're done."

Brandt watched as Xander and Seaton silently moved onto the porch, while David and Evan prowled around to the back of the house. It seemed the trackers were going to go in through both entrances to keep them from escaping. Brandt only hoped they made the men suffer, and while he'd never condoned violence against women, he wouldn't be opposed to them getting a little rough with Rebecca as well. After everything she'd done to Falan, she deserved it.

His heart was pounding in his chest as he watched them enter the house. There were shouts inside and the sounds of bodies slamming into furniture and against the walls. It seemed to take forever, but finally, all was quiet and Xander stood outlined in the doorway, motioning for them to enter the house. Brandt and Nolen rushed across the yard and into the house. The two men who'd help capture their mate were out cold, and Rebecca was forcibly held on the floor by Seaton.

"She's back here," Evan said from the hallway. "It's the bedroom on the right. I only peeked in because I didn't want to frighten her."

Brandt tried to slow his steps. He didn't want to go bursting into the room and scare her to death. He pushed the door open and looked into the darkened room. His heart constricted in his chest. Tied up in a corner on the floor, her blouse torn, blood dripping down her arms from various cuts, she was the most beautiful sight he'd ever seen.

He knelt beside her and smoothed her hair back from her face. There was a long gash across one cheek and the corner of her mouth was swollen and bloodied. He quickly untied her hands and feet and pulled her into his arms. Nolen knelt on her other side, obviously want to hold her. Brandt hated to relinquish her, but he allowed Nolen to gently take her from him.

Her eyes fluttered open and she looked at both of them. "I worried that I'd never see you again."

Brandt felt his eyes tear, but he fought to hold them back. He could only imagine how scared she must have been. Other than being beat up, she seemed to be all right, but he had to make sure.

"Falan, baby, did they… did they touch you?"

She reached for his hand. "They tore my clothes, cut me, smacked me around a little. They told me of the horrible things they were going to do to me before they killed me, but they never got around to it."

He kissed the back of her hand and gently squeezed her fingers. With a nod to Nolen, he stood, lifting Falan in his arms and followed Nolen out of the horrible house. When they passed through the living room, Brandt saw that Hayden and Seamus had arrived. Rebecca's arms had been bound behind her and she looked at Brandt beseechingly.

"I did it for you," she told him. "I did all of it for you. You were supposed to be mine!"

Brandt growled. "I was never yours. Not once did I give any indication that I was interested in you in that way. Why you thought killing my mate and my unborn child would endear you to me, I have no idea. I hope you get what you deserve."

Without another word, Nolen watched his brother stalk out of the room. Nolen looked at the occupants one last time before following his twin. When he stepped outside, he saw that someone had brought his truck. Brandt was already climbing into the passenger seat with Falan firmly planted in his lap. Left with no choice but to drive, Nolen got behind the wheel and headed for home.

Chapter Eight

Falan stared up at her two men, both of whom were hovering and had been since they'd gotten home after a quick trip to the E.R. Three of her wounds had needed stitches. Thankfully, the guys had asked the nurse to put waterproof bandages over them because they'd insisted on a hot shower when they'd gotten home, and of course, had climbed in to help. Nolen had shampooed and rinsed her hair, taking his time and massaging her scalp. Brandt had lathered her body, gently washing the blood from her arms and face, his touch so soft she barely felt it.

"I'm so sorry, sweetheart. This never should've happened to you," Nolen said, caressing her undamaged cheek.

She placed her hand over his. "Rebecca was a sick woman, one who was obsessed with Brandt. That isn't anyone's fault and I don't blame either of you for what's happened."

Brandt kissed the back of her neck. "I'm going to leave the two of you alone for a minute. I'll have a robe waiting for you when you get out."

She nodded and focused her attention on Nolen.

He fingered her sore lip, his expression tender. "You have no idea how much I'd love to kiss you right now."

"So kiss me."

He shook his head. "I'd only end up hurting you. You've been through enough today."

"Nolen, please kiss me. I need you to hold me, to know that everything is going to be okay. After everything I've been through today, I don't want you to pull away from me."

He wrapped his arms around her and pulled her close. Slowly, he lowered his head to hers and kissed her gently. His lips softly caressed hers, and while her lip hurt, she wouldn't have traded Nolen's kiss for anything in the world. She buried her fingers in his hair, holding him to her. Feeling his cock pressing against her, hard and ready, she wanted him, wished he would take her. She reached between their bodies and grasped the rigid length, making him groan.

"Falan, we can't."

"Why not?"

"Sweetheart, you've been hurt. You might pull out your stitches."

"Are you seriously going to tell me no sex until my stitches come out in a week?"

He looked rather pained, but he nodded. "That's what I'm telling you. It's not going to be easy for us, either, but it's what's best for you right now."

She wanted to growl in frustration. "And what if I want you despite my stitches?"

He cupped her cheek and smoothed his thumb over her uninjured cheek. "No matter your wishes, we will not bend on this. Your health and well-being are of utmost importance to us."

Falan sighed and rested her head against his chest. She wanted to be angry with him, but it was impossible, not when he was being so dear. She would just have to be content the next few days being held in their arms and lying between them.

He smoothed her hair back from her face, his eyes tender and caring. "There's something I've wanted to say to you since our first time together, but the moment never seemed right. I'm not even sure *this* is the right moment, but when I thought I'd lost you and hadn't told you…"

"Told me what?"

He pressed his lips to hers once more. "I love you, Falan, more than anything in this world. The thought of losing you nearly destroyed me, but knowing that I'd never told you how I felt, that made it even worse. My mind kept going through horrible scenarios of what was happening to you and it tore me apart knowing that you had no clue how I felt about you, that you were going through that alone, not knowing that I love you more than life itself."

She cupped his cheek. "I love you, too, Nolen. So very much."

He turned into her hand and kissed her palm. After gazing into one another's eyes a moment longer, Nolen turned off the water and helped Falan out of the shower. She found herself wrapped in a towel the moment her feet touched the bathmat and smiled up at Brandt.

"He's not the only one who's fallen under your spell," Brandt told her. "I think I began falling in love with you the moment I saw you sitting across the room that night. You were so beautiful that I couldn't imagine why no one was asking you to dance, and then I realized it was my good fortune that no one had because it allowed me to sweep you off your feet."

She placed her hands on his chest. "I was so overwhelmed when the two of you came to my table that night. I'd never had such good looking men take notice of me before. And then later, when I needed your help, you came running. I think I started falling in love with you that night."

He kissed her gently. "I love you, baby, and I always will."

"I love you, too, Brandt."

Nolen pressed close to her back and placed his hand over her stomach. "We need to get dressed so we can feed you and the baby. You missed dinner."

Falan understood their reasoning behind waiting a week, she really did, but what if she didn't want to wait a week? She wondered just how far she could push them, just what would it take to make them come around to her way of thinking? With a gleam in her eye, she fell to her knees in front of Brandt and jerked his boxers down. He looked stunned and before he had time to recover, she took him in her mouth, enjoying the long, hard length of him. He groaned and sank his fingers into her hair.

"Falan, stop baby. We can't do this right now."

She looked up at him through her lashes and slid her lips down his shaft again. She felt Nolen sink down behind her, his legs embracing her as his hands caressed her sides and then slid around to cup her breasts. She could feel his hard cock pressing against her, begging for entry.

Falan grabbed Brandt's ass and pulled him closer, sucking him all the way to the back of her throat. Nolen's hand glided down her body and down between her legs. He parted the lips of her pussy and teased her clit with his fingers, moving them in small tight circles. Wanting more, she spread her legs and rose further on her knees, hoping he would pick up on her hint and take her.

Her lips moved rhythmically over Brandt's cock as Nolen teased her. She felt herself getting tighter, every nerve on fire, and then she was exploding. She moaned around Brandt's cock as she tumbled into orgasm. Her body was still trembling when she felt Nolen grasp her hips and enter her slowly. As he moved in and out of her, she found herself mimicking his motions, letting Brandt's cock slide over her tongue again and again.

Nolen pushed her hair aside and trailed kisses from her shoulder to her neck, where he gently nipped her. It made her shiver and she sucked on Brandt harder. Nolen plunged into her deeper and faster, pushing both of them to the brink. The closer he pushed her to orgasm, the more frantic her motions with Brandt, until he cried out and came, bathing her throat with his seed.

She swallowed every drop and still held onto Brandt, scared to let go else she fall. Her legs trembled and her hands shook. Her breath was fast and shallow, her eyes mostly closed. Just when she thought she couldn't take anymore, Nolen thrust into her last time, triggering her release, and they came together.

Brandt knelt before her and smoothed her hair back from her face. "That was a very bad girl."

She grinned. "I don't recall you complaining a moment ago."

Nolen wrapped an arm around her waist and held her close. "Sweetheart, it isn't that we're complaining, exactly, but you could have hurt yourself."

She held her arms up for inspection. "But I didn't, see?"

Brandt gently took her arms and studied them. "I don't see any blood seeping through the bandages, but that doesn't mean you couldn't have pulled a stitch. You might have gotten your way this time, but no more. Not until those stitches come out."

She sighed and tipped her head back to rest it against Nolen's chest. "Fine. But you can't really blame me."

Brandt arched an eyebrow. "We can't?"

"You can't tell me that you love me and not expect me to show you how much I love you. Telling you wasn't good enough."

Brandt sandwiched her between them and kissed her deeply. "Baby, we love it when you show us how much you love us, and we love showing you, as well. We just ask that you stick to words for a few more days."

She nodded. "Words are good."

He smiled. "I love you, Falan."

"So do I, sweetheart," Nolen rumbled behind her.

"And I love both of you, more than I ever thought possible. Who'd have ever thought my favorite place to be would be between two wolves?"

The brothers grinned and kissed her once more. And the three of them knew there would always be "one more." One more lingering look, one more touch, one more kiss.

About the Author

Jessica Coulter Smith has lived in various places around the US, from Georgia to California. She currently resides in Tennessee. An author of adult romance and YA romances (under Jessie Colter), she began her writing career as a poet. Her first poem was published when she was 16, but that was just the start. Many published poems later, along with an Editor's Choice Award for "My World is Tumbling Down", she is quickly making a name for herself as a novelist.

When she isn't writing, Jessica enjoys spending time with her family, reading, or going to the beach. She's also an avid horse lover and owns an American Saddlebred gelding, who occasionally needs to be reminded he's not a dog.

Jessica loves to hear from her fans! You may email her at JessicaCoulterSmith@yahoo.com or visit her at her website: http://www.jessicacoultersmith.com/.

Printed in Great Britain
by Amazon.co.uk, Ltd.,
Marston Gate.